T

Affair

Made in Savannah
Cozy Mystery Series Book Nine

Hope Callaghan

hopecallaghan.com
Copyright © 2018
All rights reserved.

***** *****

This book is a work of fiction. Although places mentioned may be real, the characters, names and incidents, and all other details are products of the author's imagination and are fictitious. Any resemblance to actual events or actual persons, living or dead is purely coincidental.

No part of this publication may be copied, reproduced in any format, by any means, electronic or otherwise, without prior consent from the copyright owner and publisher of this book.

Visit my website for new releases and special offers: hopecallaghan.com

Thank you to these wonderful ladies who help make my books shine - Peggy H., Cindi G., Jean P., Wanda D. and

Barbara W. for taking the time to preview *The Family Affair,* for the extra sets of eyes and for catching all of my mistakes.

A special THANKS to my reader review teams, here in the U.S., and those across the pond, over the border and an ocean away!

Alice, Amary, Barbara, Becky, Becky B, Brinda, Cassie, Charlene, Christina, Debbie, Dee, Denota, Devan, Grace, Jan, Jo-Ann, Joeline, Joyce, Jean K., Jean M., Katherine, Lynne, Megan, Melda, Kat, Linda, Lynne, Pat, Patsy, Paula, Rebecca, Renate, Rita, Shelba, Tamara, Valerie and Vicki.

Allie, Anca, Angela, Ann, Anne, Bev, Bobbi, Bonny, Carol, Carmen, David, Debbie, Diana, Elaine, Elizabeth, Gareth, Ingrid, Jane, Jayne, Jean, Joan, Karen, Kate, Kathy, Lesley, Margaret, Marlene, Patricia, Pauline, Sharon, Sheila and Susan.

CONTENTS

Cast of Characters

Carlita Garlucci. The widow of a mafia "made" man, Carlita promised her husband on his deathbed to get their sons out of the "family" business, so she moves from New York to the historic city of Savannah, Georgia. But escaping the family isn't as easy as she hoped it would be and trouble follows Carlita to her new home.

Mercedes Garlucci. Carlita's daughter and the first to move to Savannah with her mother. An aspiring writer, Mercedes has a knack for finding mysteries and adventure.

Vincent Garlucci, Jr. Carlita's oldest son and a younger version of his father, Vinnie is deeply entrenched in the "family business" and is not interested in leaving New York.

Tony Garlucci. Carlita's middle son and the first to follow his mother to Savannah. Tony is protective of both his mother and his sister, which is a good thing since the Garlucci women are always in some sort of a predicament.

Paulie Garlucci. Carlita's youngest son. Mayor of the small town of Clifton Falls, NY, Paulie never joined the "family business," and is content to live his life with his wife and young children far away from a life of crime. Gina, Paulie's wife, rules the family household with an iron fist.

Chapter 1

Carlita Garlucci grabbed the pepper grinder and twisted the knob, coating the top of the chicken breasts in a thick layer of black pepper.

"Ma!" Mercedes yanked the pepper grinder from her mother's hand. "You're drowning the chicken in pepper. We're making Tuscan chicken mac and cheese, not pepper-flavored chicken."

She scraped a layer of pepper off the chicken and reached for the shaker of salt. "You gotta relax. Vinnie should be here any minute now and then you can stop worrying about whatever it is that has you worried."

"And not a moment too soon," Carlita groaned. "You know how I hate surprises. I wish he would've just told me what his surprise was instead of making me wait."

She thrust her hand on her hip and watched as her daughter turned the chicken over and began seasoning the other side. "He's actin' all suspicious. I know my son and I know when something ain't right."

She trudged to the other side of the apartment and to the French doors, leading out onto the balcony. "Ever since he started hinting around about moving up in the 'family business,' my gut has been churning."

"It will all be over soon enough. I'll finish cooking the chicken if you want to mix some Italian dipping sauce for the bread. I think you'll like the latest version I've been tweaking." Mercedes reached behind the spice rack and handed her mother a recipe card.

Carlita studied the recipe. "I don't think Vinnie likes parsley."

"He won't even know it's in there." Mercedes changed the subject. "I see Bob Lowman and his men have finished ripping out the walls between the front part of the restaurant and the back section."

"Ravello," Carlita's dream restaurant, was well on its way to becoming a reality. After Christmas, Carlita, along with Mercedes and her son, Tony, had traveled to Atlanta to sell several of their larger gems to a big pawnshop in the metro area.

The gems had given Carlita enough cash to fund the entire restaurant renovation project. With cash in hand, Carlita and Lowman met with an architect and engineer to go over her vision for the gourmet Italian restaurant.

After meeting to finalize the plans, the architect had taken them to the city building department and the SAS, or Savannah Architectural Society, for the necessary approvals, because of the building's historic designation.

Glenda Fox, a member of the SAS and Carlita's friend, was instrumental in getting the

SAS approval for the renovations. The city building department was another story.

The head of the building department required several changes to the plans. When Carlita was beginning to wonder if they would ever get the renovation project off the ground, the plans were finally approved.

As soon as Bob Lowman taped the construction permit in the front window of the building, he and his crew began demolition on the interior. Before tearing everything out, mother and daughter had taken on the tedious task of removing as many of the antique light fixtures, porcelain doorknobs and even the pieces of crown molding that they could salvage.

Mercedes had also tackled the time-consuming project of removing layers of old paint, so the pieces of molding looked new again.

"It's shaping up nicely," Carlita agreed as she pulled a block of parmesan cheese from the refrigerator and set it on the counter.

She stepped over to the cutting board and reached for a large carving knife to slice a lemon. "Speaking of shaping up nicely, how's your new novel coming along?"

Mercedes frowned. "It's not. I've hit another dreaded writer's block. I need some inspiration, some sort of shocking crime with a twist. I also need a crazy character to spice things up."

Carlita snorted. "I have the perfect character. Go spend a couple hours with Elvira and her sister, Dernice. They'll give you enough fiction fodder for an entire series."

"That's an idea," Mercedes brightened. "The chicken is ready. Now what?"

Carlita finished mixing the spices and began working on the chicken mac and cheese recipe. She attempted to keep the conversation light, but all the while, the nagging suspicion Vinnie's surprise was going to be more of a bombshell hung over her head like a dark cloud.

It was unlike her eldest son to cancel plans last minute like he did at Christmastime and he'd been very evasive. Finally, Carlita asked him point-blank what was going on, and he refused to tell her what he'd been up to.

She'd even asked her middle son, Tony, to try to weasel the information out of his older brother.

Tony's attempt failed. Vinnie refused to elaborate on his recent whereabouts and his big surprise, which worried Carlita even more.

Mercedes interrupted her mother's musings. "You think it's the family, don't you?"

Carlita released a heavy sigh and slowly nodded. Despite her promise to her husband, Vinnie, Sr. on his deathbed that she would get their children out of the "family," breaking all ties with the New York mafia, she'd only been partially successful.

Carlita's youngest son, Paulie, had dabbled in the "family" business years ago, before changing his mind. He married his college sweetheart, Gina, and was now mayor of Clifton Falls, a small town in upstate New York.

Tony had gone the way of his father and become a member of the "family," but she'd managed to convince him to join Mercedes and her after they moved to Savannah, and it had worked out perfectly.

Life had done a complete reversal for Tony. He'd begun dating one of Carlita's tenants, Shelby Towns, who lived in Carlita's building with her adorable daughter, Violet.

Carlita was adamant about not prying into her son's personal life, but she noticed signs that the relationship between Tony and Shelby was getting serious.

Her biggest worry and the biggest concern was her eldest son, Vinnie, who was all in with the "family."

Only a few short months ago, Vinnie had been on the run from one of the mob bosses after giving him some bad information. The incident had given Carlita a glimmer of hope Vinnie would come to Savannah and forget about the family and his past life. Her hopes were dashed when Vinnie returned to New York.

"I think you should invite Autumn to dinner."

Mercedes gave her mother a quick look. "To see if there's still a spark of interest between Vinnie and Autumn?"

"It wouldn't hurt," Carlita shrugged. "Why don't you send her a text?"

"Sure." Mercedes handed her mother the wooden spatula. "I'll be right back."

Carlita dumped the cooked pasta in the colander and turned her attention to mixing the sauce. Not only had Vinnie been mysterious about his whereabouts and his surprise, he refused to commit to staying in Savannah for any length of time, answering only in vague, short sentences.

Maybe she was being paranoid, but Carlita got the feeling when she was talking to Vinnie there was someone else nearby, listening in on the conversations.

Her heart skipped a beat as it dawned on her that perhaps Vinnie suspected his cell phone was being tapped or his home had been bugged. Maybe Vinnie was in serious trouble and was too afraid to tell his mother what was going on.

A knot formed in her stomach and visions of Vinnie being gunned down in broad daylight ran through her head. She squeezed her eyes shut. *Don't go there, Carlita,* she scolded herself.

"She can't." Mercedes popped back into the kitchen and Carlita jumped. The mixing spoon flew out of her hand and hit the floor with a loud clatter as a spray of white pasta sauce spattered the front of the stove and Carlita's apron.

"Oh my gosh. I'm sorry. I didn't mean to scare you." Mercedes snatched the spoon off the floor and dropped it into the sink.

Carlita grabbed a paper towel and joined her daughter as they wiped the droplets off the front of the stove and the floor. "It's okay."

Rambo, Carlita's pooch, trotted into the room and licked a splotch of pasta sauce they missed. Carlita patted his head. "Rambo to the rescue. You're our crumb picker-upper."

The pooch licked Carlita's hand and then inspected the rest of the kitchen floor to make sure they hadn't missed another spot.

"Autumn can't make it and I have some bad news."

"I hope she's okay."

"She's fine. She has a date with a firefighter who lives in her apartment building. Cole something."

"I guess we can scratch Autumn off the list of eligible ladies in Savannah to entice Vinnie to stay." Carlita's phone began to chirp and she snatched it off the kitchen counter. "It's Vinnie.

He said he just got off the highway and stopped to get gas. He should be here in about half an hour."

Carlita texted her son back, telling him to drive safely and then turned her attention back to the pan on the stove. "You wanna run downstairs and tell Tony his brother is getting close? Tell him we'll have dinner right after the pawnshop closes."

"Sure. I'll be back in a sec." Mercedes darted out of the apartment, slamming the door behind her.

Carlita jumped again, muttering under her breath. Vinnie couldn't get there soon enough and maybe that was all Carlita needed...to see her son, hug him tight and reassure herself he was all right.

Sudden tears burned the back of her eyes. Soon, it would be the first anniversary of her Vinnie's sudden death. Maybe that was what was wrong...Carlita was spending more time reflecting on Vinnie's unexpected passing.

She'd tried hard not to dwell on him not being with her anymore. Carlita knew her husband would be proud of her for all she'd accomplished on her own, not to mention her unwavering resolve to keep their children safe.

It didn't ease the emptiness she felt when she crawled into bed alone. The previous night, she caught herself sliding her hand across the bed to the other side, wishing that just once more she would grasp the warm and worn hand, so much like her own.

She could almost hear Vinnie's gravelly voice, speaking softly to her in the stillness of the night, calling her by her middle name. *Aw, Lenore, you gonna get all mushy on me now?*

A small smile played on Carlita's lips. *Vinnie, you oughta tell me once in a while how I'm still your girl, romance me like the old days.*

Vinnie would always pull Carlita to him, wrapping both arms around her as he nuzzled her neck. *You're gonna turn me into an old softie yet.*

A tear trickled down Carlita's cheek and she hastily swiped at it. There was no time to go soft now. Carlita had responsibilities, a family to take care of...starting with Vinnie, Jr.

The front door banged shut and Mercedes jogged into the kitchen. "He's here," she said breathlessly. "I saw Vinnie's car pull into the alley."

Carlita gave the sauce a quick stir and turned the burner off. She lifted her apron off her head before smoothing her hair. "Let's go down and help him with his bags."

The sadness over Vinnie faded as she shoved her feet into a pair of flats and followed Mercedes down the stairs and onto the alley stoop.

Mercedes and Carlita hurried to the other end of the alley and the apartment parking lot. She could see Vinnie's tall, thin frame emerge from the driver's side of the car.

The passenger side door slowly opened.

Mercedes instinctively slowed as she reached out and clutched her mother's arm. "Who is *that?*"

Chapter 2

Carlita watched a tall, thin blonde emerge from the front passenger seat of Vinnie's sedan.

Vinnie quickly made his way to the other side of the car while the young woman wiggled out of the car, teetering precariously on hot pink stiletto heels. She swayed slightly and giggled.

"Careful." Vinnie smiled at the woman and slipped an arm around her waist to steady her.

"Oh Vin, what would I do if you weren't here to sweep me off my feet?" The platinum blonde's long black eyelashes fluttered as she placed a hand on Vinnie's chest.

"Vin?" Mercedes whispered.

"This must be our surprise," Carlita grunted. She stepped across the alley to greet her son. "Son, I'm so glad you finally made it."

Vinnie released his grip on the young woman and hugged his mother tightly. "It's good to see you, Ma." He held her at arm's length. "You look good, Ma. The balmy weather and ocean breezes agree with you."

Mercedes nudged her way in. "No thanks to you. You've given Ma gray hairs, worrying her half to death after not showin' for Christmas and falling off the face of the earth these past few weeks."

"I love you, too," Vinnie grinned as he gave his sister a quick hug. He shifted to the side and placed a light hand on the young woman's arm. "Ma, this is Brittney. Brittney, this is my Ma and my little sister, Mercedes."

Brittney smiled and in a soft voice asked, "How do you do?" She extended her left hand and the sunlight glinted on a large diamond ring on Brittney's third finger.

Carlita paused for a fraction of a second, and then caught herself as she forced a smile and took the woman's hand. "It's a pleasure to meet you, Brittney."

She stepped to the side and Mercedes grasped Brittney's hand. She didn't release her grip, instead lifting Brittney's hand for a closer inspection of the sparkler. "What a gorgeous ring. If I didn't know better, I would say this looks like an engagement ring and wedding band."

Brittney tapped her spiked heel on the gravel, the smile on her face widening to show a flawless set of bright white teeth. "It's my wedding set." The smile faded slightly and she gave Vinnie a puzzled look. "They don't know?"

Vinnie's cheeks reddened. "I...uh. I wanted to surprise my family."

A wave of dread washed over Carlita as she narrowed her eyes, studying her son's expression. "Yes, you mentioned a big surprise." It started to sink in...the sudden change of plans over the holidays, the unanswered phone calls. The big surprise was Brittney.

Vinnie clasped the woman's hand. "Brittney and I married on Christmas Eve."

Carlita blinked rapidly, trying to digest the news of her eldest son's announcement.

"I thought you would be happy." Brittney's lip trembled and she looked as if she was going to start crying.

"I...we are." Carlita quickly recovered and patted her daughter-in-law's arm. "It is a surprise. I had no idea, but I'm thrilled." She turned to Mercedes. "Right Mercedes?"

"Right." Mercedes cleared her throat. "Congratulations. Welcome to the family. I'm only sorry we weren't invited to the wedding." She gave her brother a pointed stare.

"Oh." Brittney pressed a hand to her chest. "Vinnie popped the question unexpectedly. I thought we would have a longer engagement, but he and Daddy got to talking and we decided to head down to Daddy's casino in Atlantic City to tie the knot."

"Atlantic City casino?" Carlita asked.

Brittney nodded. "Yes, we got married at Treasure Cove Casino, the casino that Daddy owns. He's making Vinnie the operations manager. Vinnie starts his new job right after we leave here. We'll be living in a penthouse apartment on the top floor and I've already started renovations."

Brittney rattled on about the casino, about Vinnie's new position, about the wedding; how she was glad that she wouldn't be too far from her parents and they were so excited Vinnie was a part of the family now.

When Brittney said the word "family," the warning bells rang in Carlita's head. She held up a hand. "Brittney, do I know your father? Is he from the Queens area?"

"Oh, I'm sure you do, Mrs. Garlucci, I mean 'Mom.'" She smiled hesitantly. "I hope it's okay if I call you Mom."

Carlita nodded. "Yes, Brittney. Now that you're a part of our family." She shot her son a sharp glance and he lowered his eyes.

"My last name is, I mean *was* Castellini."

Carlita stared blankly at her daughter-in-law. "The only Castellinis I know are Vito and Francesca."

Brittney's head bobbed up and down. "Those are my parents."

"They're..."

Vinnie quickly cut in, realizing what his mother was about to say. "They're great in-laws and we'll all get reacquainted soon."

"How soon?" Mercedes shot back.

Brittney answered. "Daddy is wrapping up a business transaction in Queens and then he and maybe Ma are heading here for a few days. Like one big happy family." She clasped her hands together, looking pleased as punch.

Carlita's head began to spin and she grabbed hold of Vinnie's car to steady herself. All of her hard work to get her family, her children away from the family had been in vain. Her eldest son not only refused to leave, he literally brought them to her doorstep. She stared at Brittney in disbelief.

"Are you okay Ma?" Mercedes touched her mother's arm.

"I'm a little dizzy," Carlita admitted. "I think I need to sit down."

"Me too," Brittney said. "It's hard to stand for too long in these shoes, although I just love them and own several pairs." She twisted her foot to show off the pink shoes. "They're Manolo Blahniks. They cost several hundred dollars and are worth every penny."

She turned her attention to Mercedes. "Vinnie told me that there's a shopping center out near the highway and he thought maybe you would have time to take me shoe shopping."

"Of course," Mercedes smiled politely and turned to her brother. "Bro, I think you should grab your luggage so we can go upstairs, before Ma passes out right here in the alley."

"Right." Vinnie turned his attention to his mother. "You want me to help you upstairs first? You do look kinda pale."

"What about me?" Brittney pouted. "I could fall and break my neck on this loose gravel."

"I'll be all right son. The initial shock, I mean, surprise is starting to wear off. You help Brittney, and Mercedes and I will grab your luggage."

"Oh, I don't think so." Vinnie popped the trunk and then lifted the lid.

Mercedes gasped as she gazed inside. Every square inch was crammed full of luggage...large pieces, small pieces. There was even a hatbox.

"It's gonna take a coupla trips," Vinnie said.

"Don't forget about the suitcases in the back seat," Brittney said.

Carlita's eyes widened as she peered into the back seat of the car. It was stacked seat-to-ceiling with even more luggage. "I don't think we're going to be able to fit these in our apartment."

"I kinda figured," Vinnie said. "I was thinkin' maybe I could rent-a-bed from one of those rental places and put it in the empty apartment, if it's still empty."

"It's still vacant. My new tenant isn't moving in until February first."

"Perfect," Vinnie beamed as he offered his arm to his wife. "We can head inside and I'll come back for the luggage."

"You and what army?" Mercedes joked.

"Very funny, Mercedes," Vinnie frowned.

The group began making their way down the alley to the back of the apartment.

Carlita caught a glimpse of a movement in the window of the building across the hall, Elvira's window.

She shifted her gaze, certain Elvira or one of her minions was watching them. Carlita opened the building's door and stepped to the side. "You should say 'hi' to your brother before going upstairs. You can introduce him to..."

Carlita's words caught in her throat. She swallowed hard and forced them out. "...introduce Tony to your new wife."

Mercedes led the way into the back of the pawnshop. Inside were several customers, along with Tony and Josh, one of the pawnshop employees.

Tony was in the front of the store, assisting a customer with his back to them.

"Oh, a jewelry case," Brittney made a beeline for the jewelry and Vinnie followed behind, leaving Carlita and Mercedes alone.

"I'm shocked," Mercedes said bluntly.

"You're shocked? I thought I was going to hit the ground," Carlita hissed under her breath. "Vinnie up and married the mob boss' daughter and not just any mob boss' daughter, but the godfather. I feel like throwin' up."

Mercedes' eyes followed the couple as Brittney gazed inside one of the display cases. "She seems a little too innocent and naïve for big bro."

"Maybe it's all an act to throw us off. She's probably been sent here to spy on us. Think about it. We know for a fact the family has been down here, checking on us. Now they won't even have to hide it. One of them is family now - literally."

A wave of nausea washed over Carlita. It was the worst-case scenario. "What was Vinnie thinking?"

"I don't know. What I do know is someone needs to have a serious conversation with him," Mercedes said. "I think that's why he kept it a secret. He knew you wouldn't approve."

"We need to warn Tony." Tony's customer exited the store and she motioned him over while Josh made his way to the jewelry counter and opened the case for Brittney and Vinnie.

Tony gave his brother a quick glance and made his way to his mother's side. "I guess the hot blonde is Vinnie's surprise."

"Wife," Carlita said.

"Wife?" Tony raised an eyebrow. "Vinnie got married?"

"Yep," Mercedes nodded.

Tony let out a low whistle. "No wonder he didn't tell you what he was up to."

"If I'd known, I would've knocked him out, tied him up and locked him in the apartment until he came to his senses."

Tony turned to study the couple. "She's a looker, kinda young though."

"My thoughts exactly," Mercedes said.

Brittney sashayed across the store. "Vinnie bought me this Tiffany watch. Isn't it fabulous?" She waved a hot pink, diamond encrusted watch in their faces. "And such a bargain, too."

Mercedes said the first thing that came to mind. "It matches your shoes."

Carlita pointed to Tony. "Brittney, this is Tony, my middle son and Vinnie's brother." She turned to Tony. "Tony, this is your new sister-in-law, Brittney."

"Pleasure to meet you." Tony shook her hand and motioned to the watch. "You have a good eye for jewelry. That's a fine piece."

Tony snaked an arm around his older brother's shoulders and gave him a man-hug. "Ma is gonna kill you," he whispered in his ear.

"Yes, it is." Brittney didn't appear to hear Tony as she smiled brightly and admired her new watch.

"Are Shelby and Violet going to join us for dinner?" Carlita asked. "I'm making Tuscan chicken macaroni and cheese."

"I hope so," Tony said. "Shelby had to work all day. I left her a message and figured she'd call me back on her lunch break. I haven't heard back. I should try again. I'm getting kinda worried."

"I'm sure she's fine." Carlita patted her son's arm. "We better head upstairs. Vinnie has a lot of luggage to unload."

"You wanna borrow my apartment?" Tony asked.

"No, they need more space," Mercedes quipped. "Their luggage won't fit inside your apartment."

Carlita pinched Mercedes' arm.

"Ouch."

"Vinnie and Brittney are going to stay in the vacant apartment since our new tenant, Mr. Ivey, won't be moving in until February."

Tony promised he would join them after the store closed and the others retraced their steps through the back of the store before climbing the stairs and making their way into their apartment.

Carlita pulled out a tray of munchies from the fridge and then started a pot of coffee while Vinnie lugged the luggage up the stairs to the empty apartment.

While the coffee brewed, Mercedes offered to track down a few pieces of furniture from the local rental place, including a bed, a sofa and a television.

Vinnie was vague on the length of time they would be staying, which left Carlita wondering how long she would have to worry about the mob showing up on her doorstep.

After Vinnie stowed the luggage, the foursome congregated at the dining room table. The conversation centered on Brittney, the new penthouse apartment and Vinnie's new job.

Brittney rattled on, giving Carlita a chance to study her. She seemed innocent, perhaps a little too innocent or maybe she had led a sheltered life, which wasn't unusual for a female "family" member.

Carlita gazed at Mercedes, remembering how Vinnie and she had attempted to shelter their daughter from the "family."

Looking back, she would've done things differently and prepared Mercedes for the real world. After Vinnie's death, Carlita and her daughter had struggled to figure out not only how to open bank accounts, but how to balance those accounts and handle business transactions.

As Brittney talked, Carlita could see the young woman was head-over-heels in love with Vinnie. She gazed thoughtfully at her son. Was Vinnie in love with her or was he using her to expand his position within the "family?"

She hoped, or at least suspected, it was some of both. Vinnie was a good son, but she was shocked by the announcement, especially after Vinnie's first failed marriage to Michele. He'd sworn off ever marrying again.

Carlita turned to her daughter. "Any luck with the furniture rental?"

"Yes. The rental place promised to drop the stuff off sometime before five o'clock. There was an extra fee, but at least Vinnie and Brittney won't be sleeping on the floor."

True to their word, a big box truck arrived an hour later, and Mercedes and Carlita helped Vinnie and his new bride settle in. It was early evening when they finished, giving Carlita just enough time to warm the Tuscan chicken dinner. She was in the process of setting the table when Tony showed up.

She took one look at her son's face and knew something was wrong. Carlita dropped the oven mitt on the counter. "What's wrong?"

"It's Shelby. She's at the Savannah-Burnham Police Department being questioned."

Chapter 3

"The police department?" Carlita's hand flew to her mouth.

Mercedes overheard the conversation and hustled into the living room. "The cops are here?"

"No." Tony ran a ragged hand through his hair. "Shelby is down at the police station. I don't have the details. She called and asked me to pick Violet up from the daycare since I'm the only one on the approved list of people allowed to pick her up."

"You better go, son. Don't worry about dinner."

Tony nodded. "I'll be back with Violet as soon as possible."

"Wait." Mercedes held up a hand. "I'll go with you. You can sign Violet out of the daycare, I'll bring her back here and then you can run over to the police department to find out what's going on."

"That's a great idea, Mercedes," Carlita said.

Mercedes grabbed her purse and followed Tony into the hall, passing Vinnie and Brittney, who were on their way over.

"Where they goin'?" Vinnie asked as the door to the apartment building slammed shut.

"There's been a small issue with Shelby. Tony and Mercedes are on their way to pick up Shelby's daughter, Violet, from the daycare. As soon as Mercedes and Violet get here, we'll eat."

"What about Tony and Shelby?" Vinnie noted the look on his mother's face and quickly changed the subject. "We got everything situated over in the apartment. Thanks for letting us hang our hats there during our stay."

"It's cozy," Brittney said.

"I'm glad you like it. Would you care for some water? Sweet tea?" Carlita asked.

"I've never had sweet tea," Brittney patted her hips. "I try not to eat too many sweets. Bad for the figure. I suppose I can try it, just this once."

Carlita filled three glasses with ice and tea, handed one to Brittney and the other to Vinnie before grabbing her own and lifting the glass. "I propose a toast."

Vinnie and Brittney lifted their glasses.

"To the family."

Vinnie lifted a brow as he clinked his glass and then took a small sip. "That was an interesting toast."

"It's been an interesting day, wouldn't you agree?" Carlita asked.

"No arguing with that."

"This tea is delicious. Is it homemade?" Brittney took another sip.

"Yes. I got the recipe from a friend who's a native southerner." Carlita took a sip.

"I'm trying to watch what I eat or drink." Brittney cast Vinnie a sly look. "Vinnie and I plan to start a family soon. We better get started if we're going to have six little bambinos before Vinnie gets too old."

Carlita choked on her tea and spewed it out.

Vinnie patted his mother on the back. "You okay Ma?"

"It went down wrong," Carlita gasped. "Did you say you want six children?"

"The more the merrier," Brittney sing-songed. "Right Vin?"

"We're still hammering out the details," Vinnie said.

"You make it sound like a business transaction."

Brittney set her drink glass on the table and tottered across the room where Rambo lay sprawled out in front of the balcony doors. "Hello, Sambo." She delicately patted the dog's head.

"Rambo," Carlita corrected.

Brittney wiped the palm of her hand on her designer jeans. "Do you mind if I step onto the balcony?" She began fanning her face. "It's a little stuffy in here."

Vinnie strode across the room and unlocked the door. "It's a beautiful day and a lot nicer than Atlantic City right now." The couple stepped onto the balcony and Carlita joined them.

"There's not much of a view," Brittney wrinkled her nose. "The apartment we're in has a much prettier view of the courtyard." The woman rattled on about the casino penthouse again and Carlita met her son's eye.

He gave her a small shrug as he eased himself onto one of the lounge chairs.

Carlita's eyes drifted to Elvira's apartment building across the alley. Dusk was setting in, and she could see a small light on in what Carlita knew to be the apartment's cramped bathroom.

Except for a casual chat with Elvira and her sister, Dernice, on New Year's Eve, there hadn't been much activity in or around her former tenant's building. Most people would think that was a good sign when one's neighbor was a busybody, but it was not necessarily the case when it involved Elvira.

Quiet could mean something completely different. In fact, it was a little too quiet. Carlita made a mental note to stop by her ex-tenant's apartment to see what she was up to when she spotted their car pulling into the alley.

Mercedes climbed out of the car. The rear passenger door shot open and young Violet bolted from the passenger seat. She skipped to the back of the car, grabbed Mercedes' hand and they began making their way to the apartment entrance.

"Hey Mercedes," Carlita waved.

"Hey Ma." Mercedes waved back and Violet began hopping on one foot. "Nana Banana, Mercedes bought me this." She thrust something in the air and Carlita squinted her eyes. "What is it?"

"Magnets."

"For the fridge," Mercedes said. "I thought it might give Violet something to do while we wait for Shelby and Tony."

When they reached the apartment, Violet ran across the living room floor and out onto the patio. "Nana, Tony went to get mommy and then later, we're going to watch my favorite movie."

"You are?" Carlita knelt down so that she was eye level with the young child. "What movie?"

Violet clapped her hands. "Frozen with Elsa and Anna."

"How could I forget Frozen is your favorite movie?" Carlita gave Violet a gentle hug. "Are you hungry? Would you like a snack?"

Violet nodded. "Can I put the letters on the refrigerator?"

"As soon as you wash up," Carlita promised.

Violet turned to go, and then noticed Vinnie and Brittney. She took a tentative step back.

"Hi, Violet. Do you remember me?" Vinnie leaned forward.

"No." Violet shook her head and reached for Carlita's hand.

"I'm Tony's brother."

"And I'm Brittney." Brittney stepped closer.

Violet's eyes darted from Brittney's face to her hot pink stilettos. "You have pretty shoes."

"Thank you," Brittney beamed. "I was wondering what the weather was going to be tomorrow. I have a few jackets still in the car and told Vinnie not to bother bringing them up unless it's going to be chilly."

"One of the local news websites is pretty accurate on their weather forecasts. I'll check it out for you." Carlita guided Violet toward the bathroom. "You better get washed up. Mercedes can help you."

Violet skipped ahead and Carlita grabbed her daughter's arm. "You hear anything else from Tony?"

"No," Mercedes shook her head. "On the way here, Violet told me her daddy was coming to visit and that she saw him at the daycare the other day."

"Oh no." Carlita knew little about Violet's father, Shelby's ex. What she did know was Shelby had been living in a women's shelter before Carlita leased her the apartment across the hall.

She hated to pry, figuring she had enough to worry about. The most important thing was that Shelby loved her daughter and was a good mother. "I wonder if this has something to do with the police questioning Shelby."

Violet skipped back into the living room. "I can't reach the soap."

"I'm coming." Mercedes followed her into the bathroom.

Carlita settled in at her computer and clicked on the local news channel's website.

Savannah's winter weather could be unpredictable, depending on which way the wind was blowing. Despite the unpredictable weather, Carlita was enjoying her first winter in the south and the downright balmy temperatures in the 60s.

"It's gonna be a little chilly tomorrow, but warming up nicely for the weekend," Carlita told Brittney. She started to click out of the site when a breaking news report flashed across the screen and the image of a man appeared.

Mercedes followed Violet into the living room. "Where did you put the alphabet magnets?"

"In my backpack." Violet dropped to her knees and began unzipping her bag.

Carlita turned the volume up as a picture of an unsmiling man popped onto the screen. The banner stated the man's body had been found in the riverfront district early that morning.

Violet let out a small shriek and pointed at the picture of the man on the computer screen. "That's my daddy."

Chapter 4

Carlita quickly clicked out of the screen while Mercedes pressed her hands to Violet's eyes and guided her into the kitchen. "That was my daddy," Violet insisted.

"How about some chocolate ice cream?" Mercedes asked. "I'll even let you scoop it into the bowl."

Violet forgot about the picture of her father as Mercedes picked her up, and they peered into the freezer. "I think Nana has some sprinkles around here somewhere."

Carlita craned her neck to make sure Violet and Mercedes were out of sight of the computer screen before clicking on it. She popped her earphones in her ears and hit the play button.

"...the city's newest homicide and the details surrounding the man's death. The local authorities are questioning several persons of interest. They are also interviewing the staff at the Journey's End, the last known place where the victim was staying. We'll give you an update later this evening during the eleven o'clock news."

The reporter moved to another story and Carlita exited the screen, her mind whirling. Shelby's ex-husband was dead!

"That was Shelby's ex?" Vinnie leaned forward and whispered in his mother's ear.

Brittney stood next to her husband, a somber expression on her face. "Poor thing. I hope Tony is able to help Shelby sort this out."

Carlita held a finger to her lips. "We mustn't let on to Violet or even Shelby what we saw. I'm sure we'll hear from Tony soon enough."

The minutes crawled and Carlita finally gave up waiting for Tony to return with Shelby and decided it was time to eat dinner.

The meal was a solemn event, except for occasional chatter from Violet as she told them about her school, her friends and how her class was going to start working on Valentine's cards.

"Valentine's Day is right around the corner," Carlita said.

"I'm making a special valentine for my mom, my daddy and even you." Violet pointed to Carlita. "Nanas get special cards."

"I can't wait to see it," Carlita said.

Vinnie reached for the pasta. "This pasta is delicious, Ma. What's in it?"

Carlita rattled off the ingredients. "Chicken breasts, elbow macaroni, light cream, garlic, some other spices and, of course, my special blend of herbs."

"It's delicious, Ma," Brittney murmured. "I'm stuffed."

"You sure?" Carlita eyed her daughter-in-law's half-eaten plate of food.

"Brittney doesn't eat much. We'll wrap it up and take it over to the apartment for later," Vinnie said.

Dinner ended and after clearing the table, Vinnie told his mother that he and Brittney were going to attempt to hook up their television. They planned to stop back later to tell everyone goodnight.

Carlita followed them into the hallway. "I hope your brother shows up soon." She eyed Shelby's apartment door. "This is terrible."

"It'll be all right." Vinnie gave his mother a hug. "Thanks for dinner, Ma. We'll stop by in a little while."

She waited until the couple disappeared into their apartment before slowly making her way into hers.

Mother and daughter worked together to wash the dinner dishes. To keep Violet occupied, they pulled a chair to the kitchen sink and put her in charge of rinsing.

When they finished, Carlita hooked Rambo's leash to his collar. "Let's take Rambo for a walk."

"Can I hold his leash?" Violet asked.

"Why don't we do it together?" Carlita suggested. "If not, Rambo will be walking you, not the other way around."

They circled the block and then decided to venture to the next block, past *Shades of Ink,* Steve Winters' tattoo shop, to the corner, past Elvira's businesses, *EC Investigative Services* and *EC Security Services.*

She glanced in the front window and spotted Elvira seated behind the desk. Carlita gave a small wave, but didn't slow her pace.

They had almost cleared the front of the building when the door flew open and Elvira sprang onto the sidewalk.

"Carlita. Hey! I thought that was you." Elvira waved. "Wait up." She hurried to join them. "Hi, Violet." Elvira patted Violet's head.

"I had ice cream before dinner," Violet informed Elvira.

"Oh. That sounds good. What kind?"

"Chocolate with sprinkles. When my mommy gets here, we're going to watch *Frozen.*"

"Sounds like fun," Elvira motioned them inside the building. "You have a minute?"

"I suppose."

Violet, Carlita and Rambo followed Elvira into the building.

Dernice was seated at one of the desks. She looked up when they stepped inside. "Hey, Carlita. I noticed you got some company. Who's the smokin' hot Italian?"

"I think you're referring to my oldest son, Vinnie. He's here visiting with his..." Carlita forced the words from her mouth. "New wife."

"Barbie?" Dernice asked.

"Brittney," Carlita corrected.

"No, she looks like Barbie, as in Barbie doll." Dernice waved her hands in and out to demonstrate an hourglass figure.

"And she looks like she's twelve," Elvira added. "How old is she?"

"I have no idea," Carlita said. "It's none of my business and it's none of your business, either," she added pointedly. "Did you drag me in here to interrogate me on my new daughter-in-law?"

"No." Elvira shook her head and gave Violet a quick glance.

Dernice caught the look. "Say Violet. I have a box of doggie treats in the kitchen. Would you like to give Rambo one?"

Violet hopped on one foot. "Yes. Rambo likes treats."

Dernice and the child walked out of the office and Elvira turned to Carlita. "I caught a spot on the evening news about some guy by the name of Robert Towns. He was found murdered in a park not far from the river." She lowered her voice. "Correct me if I'm wrong. Wasn't Shelby's ex-husband's name Robert?"

"It was."

"They said they were questioning persons of interest. What's Shelby's take?"

"I don't know," Carlita answered honestly. "I haven't discussed it with her yet."

Elvira's eyes widened. "You have Violet. Shelby is down at the police station, isn't she?"

"That's none of your business."

Carlita's cell phone beeped. She pulled it from her pocket and glanced at the screen. It was a text from Tony, telling his mother he was waiting for her in the apartment.

"We've gotta run." Carlita glanced past Elvira. "Violet, it's time to go."

Violet, Rambo and Dernice joined them.

"It's time to go home," Carlita said.

"Rambo says thank-you for the doggie treats," Violet said.

Elvira followed them to the door. "I'm gonna swing by your place tomorrow. I think I may be able to help."

"I hope we won't need it." Carlita and Violet stepped onto the sidewalk, circled around the side of the building and made their way past the parking lot and Tony's car.

She held the door for Violet and Rambo, and followed them up the steps. When they reached the apartment, Carlita whispered a quick prayer that Tony wasn't alone and Shelby was with him.

If not, she had no idea what she was going to say to Violet.

***

Carlita herded Violet into the apartment where Tony was pacing near the balcony doors. "You're alone."

"Shelby is home," Tony said in a clipped voice. "You can take Violet over there. Shelby is waiting for her."

"Okay." Carlita turned to Violet. "Grab your backpack off the couch and I'll take you home."

Violet darted to the other side of the room and hugged Tony. "Bye-bye Tony Baloney."

Tony smiled as he hugged the small child. "Good-bye Violet."

"What's up with the nicknames?" Carlita ruffled Violet's hair. "I'm Nana Banana and Tony is Tony Baloney."

"Because it's funny." Violet skipped across the hall and opened the apartment door, which surprised Carlita. Shelby was always careful to keep her front door locked at all times.

She followed Violet into the apartment. "Shelby?"

A pale Shelby emerged from the hall and met Carlita near the door.

"Mommy." Violet ran across the room. "Nana and I walked Rambo and Dernice gave him treats. I ate chocolate ice cream before dinner and there's a pretty lady visiting Nana."

"There is?" Shelby kissed her daughter's cheek. "It sounds like you had fun at Nana's house."

Violet nodded. "Can we watch our movie now?"

"We can in just a minute. You go get it ready. I need to talk to Nana." Shelby motioned Carlita into the hall and pulled the door closed behind her, leaving it open a crack. "Thank you for taking care of Violet."

"I normally don't like to stick my nose in my children's affairs, but what is going on?" Carlita asked bluntly. "Tony is across the hall, wearing a hole in my floor. You're white as a ghost and Violet said her daddy is coming for a visit." She didn't mention the news clip on television. She wanted to hear what Shelby had to say.

Shelby briefly closed her eyes and then opened them. "My ex, Robert, managed to find Violet and me."

Carlita interrupted. "I know you came from a women's shelter, and I never felt it was my place to ask, but do you have a restraining order?"

"No." Shelby lowered her gaze. "I started the process. Before I finished filing the papers, Robert and I reached an agreement. He promised he would leave the area if I didn't pursue the restraining order. Everything was going fine until he contacted me, insisting we meet. He said he was working on some big deal with some important people and was going to give me a signed consent to terminate parental rights in exchange for cash."

"Where is Robert now?"

Shelby glanced over her shoulder and inside the apartment. "He's dead. Someone shot him in a park not far from the riverfront district."

"Surely, this doesn't involve you."

"It does. I agreed to meet him this morning and that's when I found his body near a clump of bushes." Shelby's lower lip started to tremble. "I called 911. After the police showed up, I went to the station with one of the officers. I've been there all day."

"They can't pin Robert's death on you because you were the one who found his body," Carlita said.

"That's what I thought too, until a couple of hours ago when one of the investigators told me they found some papers in Robert's pocket. He planned to petition the court for custody of Violet. He lied to me."

Shelby began to shake. "I'm going to prison for a murder I didn't commit. Who will raise Violet?"

Carlita's heart went out to Shelby and she placed an arm around her shoulders. "The authorities will get to the bottom of this. They can't convict an innocent woman."

"You weren't there. The investigators were talking as if the case was already wrapped up. All they need to do now is put the cuffs on me." Shelby buried her face in her hands.

"You need to get a grip. Violet needs you right now and falling apart isn't going to help." Carlita's mind spun as she tried to wrap her head around what Shelby was saying. "Tomorrow, after you've had a good night's sleep, you can come over and tell us everything you know."

"I don't want to involve you in my mess," Shelby sobbed. "It's useless. I need to plan for Violet's future without her mother."

"Nonsense," Carlita insisted. "We'll get to the bottom of it. I'm sure Tony will do all he can to help, too."

Shelby lifted her head, her tear-stained cheeks breaking Carlita's heart. "Tony won't help. On the way home, I tried to explain to him why I met with Robert. I wasn't trying to get back with him, but he was mad. He said I never should've agreed to meet with Robert alone and he couldn't trust me any longer."

Carlita stared at the young woman in disbelief. "He said that?"

Shelby nodded, her face crumpling. "I don't blame him. I should've told him from the beginning about Robert. I didn't want him involved."

"My sons have a lot of pride. They got that from their father. He was angry because he felt you didn't trust him and said whatever came to mind. I'll have a talk with him."

Carlita stiffened her back. "Now you need to go inside and spend time with Violet. She missed her momma. As soon as you get out of work tomorrow, we'll meet to go over everything you know."

Shelby sucked in a shaky breath. "That's another thing. I don't have to work tomorrow. The post office put me on indefinite leave, until the authorities clear my name."

"Oh dear. This is getting dire."

"It's hopeless," Shelby whispered.

"No, it's not. Challenging? Yes. Hopeless? Not by a long shot." Carlita walked Shelby back inside the apartment. "Let's meet at nine tomorrow morning. In the meantime, Tony and I are going to have a talk."

Carlita gave the young mother an encouraging smile and then made her way back inside her apartment, where she spied her son standing on the balcony, smoking a cigarette. "Tony Garlucci...I need to have a word with you."

Chapter 5

"Shelby made it perfectly clear she doesn't want me involved in her business and I'm not gonna force myself on someone who doesn't trust me," Tony repeated for the second time.

"Son, Shelby has a lot on her plate. She didn't want to involve you and my gut tells me there's more to the story. I'm thinkin' maybe she was trying to protect you."

"It's my job to protect her." Tony began pacing the deck. "Bottom line is that words were said neither one of us can take back."

Carlita glanced at her watch. "Shelby and I are going to get together in the morning to try to figure out what happened to her ex."

"He got offed and it's apparent someone was trying to set Shelby up to take the fall. She was the one who agreed to meet him." Tony's face reddened. "What was she doin' hanging around her ex?"

"She told me she was going to pay him money in exchange for a signed consent to get rid of him." Carlita quickly realized how that sounded. "I don't believe for a minute Shelby gunned down Violet's father."

"You got your work cut out for you on this one," Tony said. "Did Shelby tell you the police found a text on Robert's cell phone where she told him he better leave her and Violet alone or else?"

Carlita's heart plummeted. "No."

"She claims she sent that to him before he demanded money in exchange for giving up his parental rights. The cops have already wrapped up the investigation and it's only a matter of time before they show up on Shelby's doorstep and charge her with Robert's murder."

"We don't have much time, then." A light rapping on the front door interrupted the conversation.

"Maybe that's Shelby." Carlita hurried to the front door. "Be nice, be civil. Shelby - and Violet – they both need you now more than ever."

Carlita opened the door a crack and then swung it open. "I almost forgot about you, Vinnie." She peered around the corner. "Where's Brittney?"

"She was complaining of a stomach ache, so she's lying down."

"I hope my food didn't upset her stomach."

"It was delicious Ma. It might have been a little rich for her, plus she eats like a bird." Vinnie patted his stomach and stepped inside. "She don't have the stomach of steel like us Garluccis." He turned to his brother. "Did Shelby make it home?"

"She did." Carlita gazed at her middle son expectantly. "You want to tell your brother what's going on?"

Tony grunted. "Shelby went to meet her ex this morning and found him dead, shot in the head, in a park not far from the river district. The police took her to the station for questioning and we're pretty sure they're going to charge her with his murder."

"So she was gonna meet her ex and someone whacked him? It doesn't make her the killer."

"The cops found a text from Shelby on his cell phone. She told him to leave her and Violet alone or else."

Vinnie let out a low whistle. "Yeah, that ain't good. You gonna help her stay out of jail?"

"He and Shelby aren't talking. I'm going to meet with Shelby in the morning to go over everything she knows."

Mercedes emerged from her room. "I thought I heard voices. Where's Brittney?"

"Brittney is in the apartment, lying down."

She punched Vinnie in the arm. "What's the big idea of running off and marrying the head of the mafia's daughter?"

"You married into the family?" Tony sputtered. "Brittney is a mob daughter? Oh, that's a good one Vin. I'm surprised you're still alive."

"Vito and I are pals," Vinnie said.

"I wasn't talking about Vito killing you. I was talking about Ma killing you."

"I wanted to. In fact, the option is still on the table. I promised your father I would get all of you out of the family and now look at what you've done. You brought the family to my doorstep. And not only the family, but Vito Castellini himself."

"Brittney told me her father is on his way down here to check out our place," Mercedes added.

Carlita crossed her arms, her attention focused on her eldest son. "What on earth were you thinkin'?"

Vinnie became defensive and bristled at his mother's harsh reprimand. "You're not giving Brittney a chance. She's a sweet woman and isn't involved in the family."

"But you are." Carlita jabbed her finger at her son. "Are you really gonna take a job working for Castellini in Atlantic City?'

Tony hooted. "Way to go, bro. You landed a job at one of Castellini's casinos?"

"One?" Mercedes raised an eyebrow. "How many does the man own?"

"He has two. Vito's son, Tommy, runs The Royal Flush Casino on the boardwalk. I'm gonna take over the daily operations of the Treasure

Cove Casino, a block off the main drag." Vinnie shrugged. "It's gonna be an easy breezy job, mainly just keeping the staff in line."

"Tell Tony about the penthouse," Mercedes said.

"Penthouse?" Tony grinned. "You got in good, didn't you?"

Vinnie returned the smile. "Got a smokin' hot wife, a cush job, swanky digs. What more could a guy want?"

"You sold your soul to the devil," Carlita muttered. "All I gotta say is there ain't much loyalty in the family. You should know that, Vinnie. You cross Vito Castellini and your job, wife and penthouse apartment won't mean squat."

"I appreciate your concern, Ma," Vinnie replied with a tinge of sarcasm. "I love my wife. I thought long and hard before popping the question to Brittney. I'm gettin' up there in years and my options for career advancement were limited. I could languish at the bottom of the family ladder or make a big move. I chose to make the move."

"You're an adult. I hope you fully understand what you got yourself into," Carlita said.

Mercedes changed the subject. "How is Shelby?"

"She's holding up." Carlita briefly explained to her daughter what Shelby told her and that she needed help. "Your brother here, the other brother, is letting his pride get in the way. He and Shelby are fighting and he's digging in his heels."

"Turd!" Mercedes whacked Tony's arm this time. "Shelby needs you. If you stand by and let her take the rap for this, poor Violet will be homeless."

"No matter what the outcome, Violet won't be homeless. We'll be here to care for her if she needs us," Carlita said. "In the meantime, I'm meeting Shelby in the morning to try to get more information and hopefully help her figure out who offed her ex."

A sudden thought occurred to Carlita and she pressed a hand to her chest. "What if..."

Mercedes' eyes widened. "What if Shelby or Violet is next."

"Now you're scaring me Ma," Tony said.

"You should be scared - for Shelby's sake."

"I'm gonna go over and try to talk some sense into her." Tony marched to the apartment door.

"You can catch more flies with honey," Carlita called out. "Shelby has been through a lot. Remember that before you open your mouth."

Vinnie, Mercedes and Carlita watched Tony exit the apartment, slamming the door behind him, hard enough to rattle the pictures on the wall.

"He's bullheaded," Vinnie joked.

"Like someone else I know." Carlita gave her eldest son a pointed stare. "I finally get Paulie and Gina on the road to reconciliation and now I've got you two to worry about."

"There's nothing to worry about with me, Ma. Life is peaches and cream."

"As long as you give your pampered bride her heart's content 24/7, you should have it made," Mercedes teased.

"You guys got Vito pegged all wrong. He's a tough guy on the outside cuz he has to act tough. Underneath, he's a real easygoing fella once you get to know him."

"You're defending the godfather, the head of the mob?" Carlita shook her head. "They either got you brainwashed or you got your head stuck in the sand."

"It's neither," Vinnie insisted. "You'll see. Once you get to know Vito and Francesca, you'll see for yourself what I'm talking about."

The front door flew open and Tony stormed into the apartment, a dark look on his face. "I knew I shoulda left well enough alone."

"What happened?" Carlita took a step forward.

"I tried to reason with Shelby and she threw me out of her apartment."

"What exactly did you say?"

"What you told me, Ma. That she needed my help and I was there to support her."

"That's all?" Carlita asked.

"Well..." Tony averted his gaze.

"And?"

"That none of this woulda happened if she woulda come clean with me from the get-go."

"Oh Tony." Carlita threw her hands up in the air. "I've had enough. I need to come to grips with the sad state of affairs this family is in. I can't believe this day." Frustrated, Carlita stomped out of the living room and slammed her bedroom door.

She paced back and forth, talking to Vinnie's picture about their sons' predicaments. More than anything, she wished her Vinnie were there to talk some sense into them, or knock a few heads together, whichever worked.

It was a terrible predicament. She wanted Tony and Shelby to patch things up and she was concerned over Vinnie's new wife and in-laws. How had all of this happened? She'd tried so hard to make a better life for all of them and it was backfiring in every way.

Her only consolation was Gina and Paulie were doing okay, and Mercedes hadn't run off and married into the family, at least not yet.

By the time she calmed down enough to leave her bedroom, the house was dark, her sons were gone and she spotted a faint light shining under Mercedes' bedroom door.

She crept to the kitchen for a glass of water and then headed back to her room.

Grayvie, Carlita's cat, followed her into the bedroom and leapt onto the end of the bed.

She absentmindedly scratched Grayvie's ears. "Grayvie, what are we gonna do with my sons?"

Grayvie's only response was to purr while butting his head against her hand before curling up in a ball and promptly falling asleep.

"I wish I could fall asleep that fast." Carlita turned off the bedside lamp, pulled the covers to her chin and stared up at the dark ceiling.

Vinnie was probably rolling over in his grave at the behavior of his two eldest sons. Somehow, Carlita had failed...failed at the only thing Vinnie asked of her as he lay there dying and that was to save his sons from the "family."

She tossed and turned all night, sleeping in fitful spurts, only to wake to the eerie feeling something bad, even worse than what she'd already been through, was about to happen.

Finally, in the early morning hours, she gave up trying to sleep, crawled out of bed and stumbled to the kitchen to start a pot of coffee.

The sound of shuffling slippers echoed in the hall and Mercedes emerged from her room.

"I'm sorry, Mercedes. I didn't mean to wake you."

"You didn't. I was already awake." Mercedes covered her mouth to stifle a yawn. "I worked on my new book for a while and then decided to call it quits early, but just laid there wide awake. I guess I'm more of a night owl."

"Which explains why you're up with me at six in the morning," her mother teased.

"Something like that." Mercedes pulled the container of coffee from the cupboard while Carlita filled the decanter with water. "I was worried about Shelby and Violet, thinking what numbskulls my brothers are being. Has Vinnie lost his mind?"

"I'm beginning to wonder." Carlita shook her head. "I don't have anything against Brittney. She seems like a sweet girl. Still, there are a million other women out there Vinnie could have married. Why her?"

"Maybe he truly does love her." Mercedes dumped fresh coffee into the basket. "We need to give her a chance, for Vinnie's sake. What's done is done."

"You're right." Carlita turned the coffee pot on. "I guess I'm still in shock. Then we've got poor Shelby. I don't know how we can help her, but we better move fast. She's convinced the police are working on her arrest warrant."

"I would like to be there when you talk to Shelby." The coffee finished brewing. Mercedes poured a cup and handed it to her mother. "We can always ask for Elvira's help."

"Bite your tongue," Carlita said. "You think we're in a bind now, let Elvira stick her nose in this. She already offered, when I ran into her last night while Violet and I were out walking Rambo."

"She has a nose for sleuthing, I'll give her that."

"She does. Thanks for the coffee." Carlita carried her coffee to the bathroom and began getting ready for the day. As she showered, she thought about Violet. What would happen to the young girl if Shelby were to be convicted of her ex's death?

At nine on the dot, Carlita and Mercedes crossed the hall and knocked on Shelby's front door. There was a small muffled sound coming from the other side. It opened a crack and then opened wider, but it wasn't Shelby who answered.

An older, gray-haired and heavyset man peered down his nose at them. "This is a no-solicitation building. We're not interested."

Chapter 6

The man started to close the door. Carlita wedged her foot between the door and the frame. "I'm not soliciting. My name is Carlita Garlucci and I own this building."

"Oh." The man turned his head. "Shelby. You got company."

Shelby appeared in the doorway. "Thank you. I can handle this."

The man grunted, giving Carlita a warning look and then limped away while Shelby joined Carlita and Mercedes in the hall. "I'm sorry. Uncle Jerry can be a little abrupt, not to mention we're all on edge."

"That...that's your uncle?" Mercedes asked.

"Yes. He showed up on my doorstep early this morning after seeing Robert's murder plastered all over the news. Actually, he *and* my aunt showed up on my doorstep."

"I've never heard you mention family nearby." Carlita said the first thing that popped into her head.

"My parents died years ago. Uncle Jerry and Aunt Ginny are the only family I have left."

"At least you have family," Mercedes said. "What do your aunt and uncle think of Robert's death?"

"They're glad he's gone. There was no love lost between Uncle Jerry and Robert. Hang on a sec." Shelby held up a finger. She slipped back inside the apartment and returned moments later. "They're going to keep an eye on Violet so we can talk in private, if you want."

"Yes, of course." Carlita led Shelby and Mercedes back inside their apartment. "Would you like some coffee?"

"No." Shelby shook her head. "I've been drinking coffee all morning."

"Have a seat." Carlita motioned to the chair. "I'm sorry you and Tony weren't able to patch things up."

"Maybe it's better this way." Shelby shifted uneasily. "I can see his point of view yet he refuses to see mine."

"Stubborn as a mule," Mercedes said. "All of my brothers, except for maybe Paulie, but he's married."

"So is Vinnie," Carlita pointed out.

"I forgot all about Vinnie and his surprise. Tony didn't mention it. Let me guess...he's decided to move to Savannah."

"I wish," Carlita said. "He got married on Christmas Eve."

Shelby's jaw dropped. "Married? And you weren't invited to the wedding?"

"He had his reasons." Carlita and Mercedes exchanged a glance. "It's a long story. Now back to your crisis. Tell me everything you think is relevant to Robert's demise."

"This might take a while."

"Take your time," Carlita said.

"I met Robert on a blind date, set up by one of my close friends. At first, he was charming, intelligent and attractive. As soon as our relationship became serious, he turned from prince charming to evil stalker. By the time I realized it, it was too late. I was pregnant with Violet."

Shelby stared at her clasped hands as she paused to gather her thoughts. "My aunt and uncle didn't approve. Of course, looking back, they could see my love for Robert was blinding me and that he wasn't a good person."

Shelby went on to tell them she told her uncle about the baby and he begged her to end the relationship. All the while, Robert begged her to sneak off and marry him.

"I was stupid and married Robert. Uncle Jerry and Aunt Ginny argued with Robert after we returned from the ceremony at city hall and ever since, I've had little contact with either of them, not because they didn't want to. After Robert and I split and I fled to the women's shelter, I felt like such a failure. I never contacted them to let them know."

"Oh Shelby." Carlita's heart went out to the young woman. "I'm so sorry. I wish we had known. It's apparent your aunt and uncle love you."

"They do." Unshed tears threatened to spill over and Shelby quickly wiped them away. "I was a fool, and as stubborn as your son."

"I hate to be morbid, but at least now you don't have to worry about Robert," Mercedes said. "Do you have any idea who might have murdered him?"

"Besides my uncle?"

Carlita studied Shelby's face. "You're not kidding."

"No. He hated Robert. I called Uncle Jerry the other day, to tell him I had left Robert some time back and now he was demanding cash in exchange for signing away his parental rights. He became enraged and said he would take care of Robert. I also asked to borrow some money, thinking the more money I had to offer my ex, the better my chances of getting rid of him for good."

"According to what you said last night, Robert planned to trick you by taking your money and then filing for custody of Violet." Carlita frowned. "Do you think he's capable of murder? Your uncle, I mean."

Shelby slowly nodded her head. "Yes, I do believe if he was angry enough or if he believed Robert was going to harm Violet or me." Shelby hurried on. "I know you're shocked and are probably wishing your son wasn't involved with a woman who has a troubled past."

"Your past is the least of my concerns. We all have a past, even us."

"Not like mine," Shelby insisted.

"You'd be surprised," Mercedes muttered under her breath.

Shelby stood. "Still, I don't think my uncle killed Robert. Robert kept talking about some big deal he was working on and trying to get me to meet him at this downtown bar, the *Black Stallion*. I've been by it before. The place gave me the creeps, even during the day."

"The *Black Stallion*." Carlita gazed at Mercedes. "Why does the name sound familiar?"

"Maybe Cool Bones mentioned it."

Cool Bones aka Charles Benson, was Carlita's other tenant. Cool Bones was a jazz singer and head of the jazz band, the *Jazz Boys*. They

82

played regular gigs at the *Thirsty Crow,* a bar in the City Market district.

"We need to ask him," Carlita said. "Is there anything else?"

"Yes. You have to promise not to breathe a word of what I'm about to say to anyone," Shelby said.

Chapter 7

"My lips are sealed," Carlita promised.

Shelby sucked in a breath. "Robert claimed he was making money hand-over-fist as a bookie. He planned to use the cash for this major deal he was working on, but he double-crossed someone with connections to an East Coast gang and they were hot on his trail. He never told me exactly what he'd done."

She cast an uneasy glance at Carlita. "On top of that, I think someone has been following me. I'm probably just being paranoid. I'm so sorry, Carlita." Shelby rubbed her brow. "The last thing I would ever want to do is bring a bunch of criminals to our doorstep. I'm considering packing a suitcase and hiding out at my uncle's house until this all blows over."

Carlita pressed the palms of her hands to her cheeks and she smiled grimly at the irony of the situation. What if Vito Castellini showed up to meet the family and was greeted by another thug who was looking for Shelby?

"You're not mad?" Shelby asked.

"Mad?" Carlita shook her head. "No, Shelby. I'm not mad. You're in a bind, and to no fault of your own." She took a step back and spun in a slow circle.

The apartment building was secure with more than enough security safeguards in place for a rental property, but if a hitman was stalking Shelby there was no place on earth where she would be safe.

"I can't tell you what to do, Shelby. Only you can make that decision. Tony and Vinnie have spent a fair amount of time around questionable characters. If you would like to stay, then I'm asking for your permission to fill them in on what you've told me."

"Tony is going to be furious."

"Maybe," Carlita conceded. "He'll get over it. I know my son and he loves you. He would never forgive himself if something happened to you."

Shelby's face crumpled and she began to cry. "I never meant for any of this to happen. I hoped and prayed after meeting with Robert yesterday, he would be out of our lives forever."

Carlita rubbed Shelby's back. "Honey, there are times when, no matter how hard you try to put the past behind you, it sneaks up and smacks you right upside the head."

"It's a mess," Shelby sighed. "I better check on Violet."

Shelby and Carlita stepped into the hall and Violet's small face appeared in the doorway. "Mommy, Papa Jerry says I have to get dressed."

"Papa Jerry is right. It's time to get dressed."

Violet gave her mother a pouty stare and disappeared from sight.

"I'm going to run inside and let my uncle know we're going to be across the hall." Shelby slipped back inside the apartment and popped out moments later. "Violet is packing. Uncle Jerry and Aunt Ginny are determined we're going to stay at their place."

She pulled the door shut behind her. "Maybe we should go to their house. They live out in the middle of nowhere, along with their guard dog, Ragnar. No one will get past Ragnar."

"As I said, I'm going to let you make that decision."

The women crossed the hall to Cool Bones' front door and Carlita rapped softly. They heard a muffled sound coming from within and then the door opened.

"Ah." Cool Bones' eyes lit. "To what do I owe the pleasure of a morning visit from two of my lovely neighbors?"

Carlita took in the sweatpants, wrinkled Duke Ellington t-shirt and flip-flops. "We're sorry to bother you. I hope we're not interrupting."

"No, not at all. Come in." Cool Bones shifted to the side. "I hope my sax practice playing isn't disrupting you."

"Never."

Cool Bones practiced on his saxophone almost every day, like clockwork, from two in the afternoon until four, but it never bothered Carlita or Mercedes. In fact, Carlita loved to listen to the haunting melodies.

Carlita followed Shelby into the apartment. "You know I love to hear you play."

"The only time I hear you play is on the weekends and only when I'm in the hall," Shelby assured him.

"Would you care for a cup of coffee? Tea?"

"I'm fine," Carlita said.

"Me too."

"Belly up to the bar ladies." Cool Bones motioned to the barstools.

Shelby ran her hand along the top of one of the barstools. It was shaped like a music note. "These are awesome."

"Thanks. My daughter, Jordan, bought them for me for Christmas."

"Ah." Carlita lifted a brow. "I forgot you left a message telling me you were in Atlanta over the holidays. It was awfully quiet around here while you were gone."

"Speaking of quiet...now that Elvira is gone, have you had any luck renting out her old apartment?"

"You mean gone from the building," Carlita joked. "Having her across the alley is almost as bad. Have you met her sister, Dernice?"

"Yes. Elvira and her sister have stopped by the *Thirsty Crow* a coupla times. Elvira introduced her to me. It was the extent of our conversation."

"Elvira and Dernice are two peas in a pod," Carlita said. "I rented her old apartment to a man by the name of Sam Ivey. He's a popular tour guide in the historic district. I've only met him once."

"Sam Ivey." Cool Bones tapped his chin thoughtfully. "I've heard the name before."

"Like I said, he's a tour guide in the area. I've seen his ads in some of the local tourist magazines. He's moving in February first."

"I look forward to meeting him. I doubt he'll give you as much trouble as Elvira did."

"I hope not."

"You say he hasn't moved in yet? I could've sworn I saw a man and woman go into the apartment last night."

"That was my oldest son, Vinnie, and his new wife, Brittney. They're here for a visit."

"Oh." Cool Bones straightened his back. "I thought your older son was single and you were tryin' to convince him to move to Savannah."

"He was single." Carlita blew air through thinned lips. "He married over the holidays. It's a long story."

"I see." Cool Bones nodded. "He surprised you with his new wife."

"More like sprang it on me," Carlita grumbled. "It's a mess."

"And none of my business. I'm sure you're not here to tell me all your family woes."

"You're right. The reason we're here is Shelby and I are looking for information on another of the local clubs, this one is in the riverfront district. I forget the name of the place." Carlita turned to Shelby.

"The name of the place is the Black Stallion Club."

Cool Bones' eyes narrowed. "The Black Stallion is no place for nice women like you. My former business partner, Smooth Sully, plays there. He quit the Jazz Boys and started his own band, the River Rats."

"What do you mean 'it's no place for nice women like you?'"

"They're a rough bunch down there. Pat, the owner, has been linked to some nefarious activities, questionable acquaintances and criminal business dealings."

"Possibly even a hangout for killers," Shelby whispered.

"Yes, ma'am." Cool Bones nodded. "Far be it from me to stick my nose in where it don't belong, but I'm gonna warn you to steer clear of the place. Why are you asking about the Black Stallion?"

"Shelby's ex-husband was trying to persuade her to meet him there and she and I were trying to figure out why."

"I don't know how you feel about your ex, but he had better watch his back if he frequents that place. If he's not careful, he'll end up pushing up daisies."

"Dead," Shelby said. "It's a little late. My ex was murdered yesterday and the authorities are trying to pin it on me."

"You don't say." Cool Bones let out a low whistle. "Let me get this straight. Your ex-husband tried to talk you into meeting him at the Black Stallion. He was murdered and now the authorities suspect you're the one who murdered him?"

"Correct." Shelby nodded. "And I think I'm being followed."

"This is quite the conundrum. At the risk of sounding nosy, do the authorities have evidence implicating you?"

Shelby laid it all out for Cool Bones, her escape to the women's shelter, her move to the apartment, how her ex had tracked her down and asked to meet with her, wanting cash in exchange for custody of Violet.

"I agreed to meet Robert in a small park not far from the river. When I got to the meeting spot, I found his body. Someone shot him."

"Did he mention anyone who might be after him?"

"He said he was working on some big deal. He also mentioned he was making fast cash as a bookie." Shelby motioned helplessly. "When he offered to sign off on his parental rights in exchange for money, I emptied my bank account, hoping to get rid of him for good."

"Tell him the other part, what the authorities found," Carlita said.

"Robert had no intention of signing away his parental rights. The authorities found a paper requesting custody instead. He was tricking me."

"Whew." Cool Bones scratched his chin thoughtfully. "I don't see an easy way out of this Shelby. What does Tony think about this?"

"We're not speaking. I never told him I was going to meet Robert, to give him money in the hopes he would go away."

"He's a hot-headed Italian, just like his father," Carlita said.

"I see. I wish I could help you, but my only connection to the Black Stallion Club is my former business partner. While you're waiting for the authorities to sort this out, I would keep a low profile. Those people down at the Black Stallion, they mean business."

A cold chill ran down Carlita's spine. It was even worse than she suspected. She reached over and squeezed Shelby's hand.

"Thank you, Charles. What you've told us has been helpful." She turned to Shelby. "Maybe you should go to your uncle's place after all."

"The farther away, the better." Cool Bones opened the door and followed the women into the hall. "I'll keep my ears open. If I hear anything at all, I'll let you know."

Carlita started to thank him and then impulsively reached out and hugged him instead. "You're a doll, Cool Bones. I don't care what Elvira says."

Cool Bones' laughter echoed in the hall and continued even after his door closed.

Shelby stared at the closed door. "I'm scared out of my mind. I've never visited anyone in jail, let alone been incarcerated." Her lower lip began to tremble.

Carlita wrapped her arms around the young woman. "I promise Shelby, I will do everything in my power to keep that from happening. You need to keep your chin up, for Violet's sake."

They walked across the hall. "If you decide to stay at your uncle's place, pop by and let me know you're leaving so I won't worry."

"I will," Shelby promised. "Thank you for everything." She reached for the doorknob before turning back. "One more thing. Could you please tell Tony I'm sorry?"

"Yes, and then I'm going to strangle him," Carlita joked.

Shelby gave Carlita a sad smile and then quietly slipped inside.

Carlita was halfway to her apartment when the downstairs doorbell chimed. She hurried down the steps. When she reached the bottom, she grabbed the knob and then peered through the peephole.

Standing on the other side of the door was a man, and he had his back to her. The man slowly turned and Carlita's breath caught in her throat.

Chapter 8

Vito Castellini's tall frame filled the peephole. Carlita watched as he lifted his gaze and cased the joint.

"Good grief." She pressed her forehead to the door and prayed she was going to survive. "When it rains, it pours," she said under her breath before yanking the door open.

Vito stood front and center on the stoop. On either side of him were two big, beefy bodyguards. One of them slid his hand into the jacket of his pinstriped suit and pulled out a gun.

"Put that away." Vito motioned to the man brandishing the weapon. "We ain't gonna shoot anyone, at least not yet." Vito shifted his attention to Carlita. A slow smile crept across his face.

"Carlita Garlucci. I bet you're surprised to see me," Vito said. "Are Vinnie and my daughter, Brittney, around?"

"Y-yes." Carlita's words stuck in her throat. "They're upstairs. Brittney mentioned you might be stopping by for a visit."

Vito shoved his hands in his pockets and looked around. "So this is the old Delmario place? You know he got whacked for double-crossing the family, right?"

Carlita wasn't sure if it was meant to be a warning. She wasn't taking any chances. "Yes. I mean, I didn't know that for certain. I've heard rumors George's killer was never caught."

Vito Castellini laughed. "And they never will. I see you're having some work done on the property. It's lookin' good. You got a pawnshop. That's a solid business venture. Vinnie told me you own rental properties, too."

"Yes, that's right." Carlita nodded. "I'll be opening a restaurant soon, Italian of course.

You'll have to come back for a visit after it opens." Carlita knew she was rambling, but Vito was making her nervous.

His henchman were staring at her as if they couldn't wait to whip out a couple of sawed off shotguns and fill her full of lead.

"Would you like to come upstairs for coffee or something..." Her voice trailed off.

"I got some business to take care of downtown, but I got a coupla minutes to spare."

"Your wife, Francesca, didn't come with you?"

"She don't like riding for long," Vito said.

"You didn't fly?" Carlita motioned them inside and began to shut the alley door when she noticed Elvira's door across the alley was ajar. It quickly closed.

"Me and my men, we can't fly with our...shall we say...extra luggage?"

"I see." Carlita reached for the handrail. "I'm sure certain items might pose a problem."

When they reached the top of the stairs, Carlita paused, offering up a quick prayer Mercedes was holed up in her bedroom. Tony was working in the pawnshop and as far as she knew, Vinnie and Brittney were in their apartment.

She led them into the apartment. The burly bodyguards made their way to the balcony doors and peered out. Vito chose to walk around the apartment.

Carlita nearly passed out when he stopped in front of the fireplace and ran the palm of his hand over the mantle...the same mantle where she'd stashed the cache of gems. "Nice fireplace."

"Thanks," she croaked. Her hand shook as she smoothed the front of her skirt. "I can't remember if you said you would like a cup of coffee."

"Yeah. Why not?" Vito never turned as he continued walking along the fireplace, studying the display of family photos scattered along the mantle.

Mercedes emerged from her room. "I thought I heard voices, Ma." She stopped abruptly at the sight of the men inside the apartment. "I didn't know we had company."

Carlita forced her voice to remain even. "Mr. Castellini, this is my daughter, Mercedes. I don't know if you ever met her."

She gripped Mercedes' arm. "Mercedes, this is Brittney's father, Vito Castellini and his...business associates."

"Hello." Mercedes' eyes widened for a fraction of a second and she turned to her mother. "Would you like me to run across the hall to let Vinnie and Brittney know her father is here?"

"I would appreciate that." Carlita attempted a smile and Mercedes headed out the door.

With no choice but to leave Vito unattended and snooping around her living room, Carlita hurried to the kitchen to start making the coffee. She quickly dumped fresh coffee into the basket, filled the coffeemaker with water and flipped the switch on.

Grrr. Rambo let out a warning growl.

Carlita had completely forgotten about her pooch and hurried into the dining room where he stood growling at the men, his teeth bared.

She darted to the other side and grasped his collar. "I'm sorry. Rambo isn't used to strangers." Carlita shooed her dog onto the balcony and shut the door behind her. She latched the doggy door so he couldn't sneak back in.

Thankfully, Mercedes returned moments later with Vinnie and Brittney.

"Daddy!" Brittney flew across the room and into her father's open arms. "I thought you weren't going to come after all. What a wonderful surprise."

"Yeah. Wonderful," Carlita muttered under her breath.

One of Vito's goons cleared his throat and pinned her with a pointed stare.

Vinnie followed his wife and extended a hand to his father-in-law. "So you decided to come down here and take care of a little business after all."

"I did." Vito nodded. "We also stopped to check on my places in Atlantic City. You still planning to head up there day after tomorrow to start work?"

"Yes, sir. We'll be in Atlantic City this Sunday evening and I'll start work Monday morning."

"Good." Vito curled his lip as he glanced around. "This place is okay. Not enough action for me, if you know what I mean. I can see how it might appeal to your Ma."

"We love it here," Mercedes said. "It's a lot safer than living in Queens."

"I wouldn't go that far," Carlita said. "I think the coffee is ready." She motioned for Mercedes to join her in the kitchen while Vinnie and Brittney chatted with Vito.

Vito's goons watched the women walk into the kitchen where they had an unobstructed view, making it impossible for Carlita and Mercedes to have a private word.

"Grab the container of pizzelle cookies and carry them to the coffee table. I'll pour the coffee."

"Sure Ma." Mercedes did as her mother asked and Carlita joined her moments later.

Vito settled in on the couch and took the cup of coffee Carlita offered. "Thanks." He took a sip before turning his attention to Vinnie. "You take care of that business matter for me yesterday?"

Vinnie gave his mother a quick glance before nodding. "Yes, sir. All taken care of."

"Good."

Carlita perched on the edge of the recliner and began silently praying that Vito wouldn't stay long.

Thankfully, Brittney chattered on about the penthouse renovations, and then rattled off the things she and Vinnie planned to do during their brief stay in Savannah.

Vito patiently listened to his daughter ramble on and then glanced at his watch before abruptly standing. "We gotta get going, Brit."

His bodyguards silently crossed the floor and stood next to the door.

"Already? You just got here," Brittney whined.

"I got some stuff to take care of." He chucked his daughter under the chin. "Me and your Ma will be in Atlantic City next week." He shifted his gaze to Vinnie. "I'm sure your new husband will have the place in ship shape condition."

Vinnie straightened his back. "Yes, sir. You won't be disappointed."

"I'm counting on it."

Brittney slipped her arm through her father's and they slowly made their way to the door. "Vinnie said once the apartment renovations are finished and we get settled in, I can get a pug and name her Petunia. Petunia the pug." Brittney giggled.

"That sounds like a real good name."

Vito and Brittney exited the apartment, followed by Vinnie, Vito's goons and Carlita. Mercedes made a move to follow, but Carlita quickly shook her head and motioned her to stay inside the apartment.

"I'll go get the car boss." One of Vito's bodyguards strode to the end of the alley where a shiny black Cadillac Escalade blocked the alley entrance.

He climbed into the driver's seat and then did a quick U-turn, pulling up alongside the back of the apartment building.

Vito's other bodyguard stepped to the rear passenger door and held it open.

"I'll see you later, Brit. Try to stay out of trouble." Vito hugged his daughter tight and turned to his new son-in-law. "I see Brit is happy. Let's keep it that way."

Vito didn't wait for a reply as he slid into the back of the luxury SUV. Vito's goon closed the door before climbing into the front passenger seat and the vehicle drove off.

Carlita waited until they were out of sight. "That was a short visit."

"Daddy doesn't stay in one place for too long. He's a very busy man." Brittney squeezed Vinnie's arm. "Daddy really likes you Vin. I can't wait for him to see our penthouse apartment when it's done."

"Me either."

A cold wind whipped around the side of the building and Brittney shivered. "Brr. It's chilly out here."

"Let's go in." Carlita started to follow the couple into the apartment when she heard someone holler her name. "Carlita!"

Carlita spun on her heel and spotted Elvira motioning wildly from her doorway. "You got a minute?"

"You guys go on ahead." Carlita walked across the alley,while Vinnie and Brittney disappeared inside.

"I see you got lots of company." Elvira nodded toward the empty alley. "That was a mighty fancy SUV that just left." She rubbed her fingers together. "We're talking big bucks. Cadillac Escalade ESV platinum version. That baby is a cool hundred k all day."

"I wouldn't know. I've never bought a new vehicle. Lots of people drive expensive vehicles." Carlita turned to go.

"Wait. That's not what I wanted to say. It's about the guy, the boss man."

Carlita raised a brow. "Boss man?"

"Yeah, the one who was calling the shots. I think I heard his henchman call him Vito."

"Yes." Carlita nodded. "His name is Vito."

"Yeah, well. I saw them come to the door earlier and the man, he looked very familiar. You know, like I've seen him somewhere."

"And?"

"I have. It took me a few minutes to figure it out." Elvira tapped her finger on the side of her head. "I never forget a face. It was last night. I saw him downtown with those two other men. I was passing by the dive, the Black Stallion over near the riverfront district, on my way to listen to Cool Bones at the Thirsty Crow. I saw them out front."

Elvira glanced over Carlita's shoulder. "I thought you might like to know I saw your son, Vinnie, too."

Chapter 9

"You're telling me that last night you saw my son, Vinnie, and the other men who just left in front of the Black Stallion?"

"Yeah." Elvira nodded enthusiastically. "And the only reason I paid attention was because the men were talking to this other guy. Now that I think about it, he reminded me of Robert Towns, Shelby's ex."

Elvira rocked back on her heels. "I did a little nosing around cuz, like I said the other day, I suspected Robert was Shelby's ex and he was."

"It doesn't mean Shelby had anything to do with her ex-husband's death."

"True. All of the information I've been able to obtain through one of my anonymous sources who works at the PD downtown leads me to believe his murder was a hired hit. Although I also heard a completely different theory and it involves Shelby."

"A hit?"

"You know," Elvira waved her hand in the air. "A professional hit, mafia style. I thought I should warn you that those men who just left might be mafia."

"You have a very vivid imagination, Elvira."

"Maybe. Maybe not. What are the chances your son shows up for a visit, the mafia-types who just left here show up and Shelby's ex-husband is murdered all within hours of each other? Yep, it sure doesn't look good for Shelby, finding her ex's body and all. I heard he was staying at the Journey's End. You ever been by that place?"

"Not that I can recall," Carlita said.

"It's not far from the river and not in the best part of town. Had a client who was staying there while he was in town. He said it was a shady joint."

"I see. I hadn't heard that tidbit of information." Carlita glanced at her watch. "I appreciate your concern over my safety, a first for sure, and I'll keep what you said in mind."

She gave Elvira a curt nod and then headed across the alley. Carlita could feel Elvira's eyes bore into the back of her head as she made her way inside. She quickly shut the door behind her and leaned her head against it.

Carlita remembered Vito pointedly asking Vinnie if he'd taken care of the "business matter." Was Robert the business matter Vito was referring to?

Had Vinnie gotten in over his head with the family? A small sharp pain pierced Carlita's temple and she began rubbing it. If Vinnie had murdered Robert, why? Why was Robert a target?

She remembered Shelby telling her that her ex mentioned making fast cash and that he was working on some sort of big deal. Did he owe the mob money? Was it Vito Castellini?

Carlita was certain Vito and his men were capable of murder, but not her son, Vinnie. Her heart told her that Vinnie was not a murderer. Her mind, on the other hand, wasn't convinced.

She knew enough about the family to know loyalty was of utmost importance. If Vinnie's new father-in-law wanted him to "take care of business," Vinnie would have no choice but to do exactly that, no matter what the "business" entailed.

She trudged up the steps, mulling over the events of the past couple of days. Carlita's world had turned upside down. Shelby and Tony were on the outs, she'd gained a new daughter-in-law, her son was in over his head with the "family" and now she had to wonder if he was a murderer.

Thankfully, the apartment was quiet when she stepped inside. Carlita needed time to come up with a plan on how to approach her son, to ask him if he was involved in Robert Towns' death.

Rambo trotted across the room and nuzzled Carlita's hand. "Let's go for a walk, Rambo. It will help clear my head."

Mercedes' bedroom door was shut and she could hear soft music coming from inside. "Hey, Mercedes. I'm gonna take Rambo to Morrell Park," Carlita hollered through the door.

She heard a muffled reply and taking it for an okay; she let Rambo lead the way to the alley. He tugged on the leash to hurry them along. They rounded the corner and nearly collided with Shelby, who was coming toward them from the opposite direction.

Both of them took a quick step back.

"Whoops. I need to watch where I'm going."

"It's okay, Shelby." Carlita shifted Rambo's leash to her other hand. "Are you all right? Your face is red."

"No. I'm so stressed out right now."

Carlita glanced around. "Where's Violet?"

"My aunt and uncle took her back to their house. We've decided to stay with them after all. I needed to take care of a few things here at the apartment."

"Does one of those things involve trying to talk to my hard-headed son?" Carlita asked softly.

Tears filled Shelby's eyes and she nodded. "Yes. I was hoping I could speak with him alone."

"Tell you what; you take a walk with Rambo and me. I think we both could use the fresh air, and when we come back I'll cover the pawnshop and give Tony a break so you and he can talk."

"You will?" Shelby brightened. "Thank you so much."

"Of course I will." Carlita squeezed Shelby's hand. "Rambo and I are on our way to Morrell Park."

The women fell into step. "I was thinking about your situation. You mentioned your ex, Robert, was working on some big deal."

"Yes," Shelby nodded. "It had something to do with Savannah because Robert planned to move back to the area."

"Where exactly did you plan to meet Robert, where you found his body?"

"It was in a small park and not far from..." Shelby's voice trailed off.

"Not far from?" Carlita prompted.

"The Black Stallion Club, now that I think about it."

Carlita checked for traffic and tugged on Rambo's leash as they crossed the street. "I'm no private investigator, but I suspect there's a link between you finding Robert's body in the park and the fact he was involved in a business transaction in the same area."

"I thought the same thing myself. Looking back, I wish I would've pressed Robert for more details on the deal he kept talking about. I figured the less I knew the better off I was." Shelby sighed heavily. "Now look at the mess I'm in. I still don't dare tell my aunt and uncle all of the details."

The women finished making their way to the park, past the Waving Girl, along the riverfront and to the ferryboat landing. The passengers finished boarding the ferry and they watched as the ferry drifted away from the dock.

"I wonder..." Carlita's voice trailed off.

"Wonder what?"

"How much time do you have?"

"Before I'm arrested?"

"No, I mean today. I was thinking we could head over to where you found Robert and have a look around." The women began retracing their steps.

"It's awful." Shelby rubbed the sides of her arms. "I still see Robert's body every time I close my eyes."

"I'm sure you do. When we get there, point me in the right direction and you can stay with Rambo while I take a closer look."

The women headed up the incline to the main thoroughfare and walked along the busy road, to the other end where the touristy part of the riverfront district began.

"I don't think I could live this close to the riverfront district. There are too many people."

Shelby nodded. "I love Walton Square and wouldn't trade it for anything."

"Me too," Carlita agreed. Rambo led the way as they circled the block. "We're running out of real estate."

"We're getting close. There's the Black Stallion Club." Shelby pointed to a brick building with a black awning.

The women continued walking and Shelby stopped abruptly in front of a sidewalk that led to a small park. "This is it. I found him over by those bushes." She pointed to a row of sprawling boxwoods. "At first, I didn't think Robert was here. When I got closer, that's when I saw him sprawled out and face down."

A tear trickled down Shelby's cheek. "It was awful. I never wanted Robert dead."

"I know, Shelby. I'm so sorry." Carlita squeezed her hand. "Did the authorities find the murder weapon?"

"No." She shook her head. "One of the investigators said the killer could've easily walked to the river and tossed it in. They tested my hands for gunshot residue. They won't find any because I didn't shoot Robert."

"Did you point that out to them?"

"Yes," Shelby nodded. "Then they said the killer could've been wearing gloves and tossed them into the river, along with the murder weapon."

"Where exactly...did you find Robert?"

"Over there." Shelby pointed to a spot between two boxwoods.

"I see." Carlita gazed around the small park. "You stay here with Rambo and I'll check it out."

Carlita handed Shelby Rambo's leash and took a tentative step toward the bushes. The grass had been trampled, but nothing else appeared suspect.

She circled the bushes, focusing her attention on the perimeter and then joined the young woman and Rambo. "I'm sure the investigators combed the place."

The women began walking up the incline.

"Wait!" Shelby's arm shot out. "I just remembered something Robert said."

Chapter 10

Shelby pointed to the street sign. "Robert mentioned Harner Street and the reason I remember it now is it reminded me of a street I grew up on - Haymark Street."

Carlita studied the street sign. She shifted her gaze beyond the sign, toward the river. "It's close to the spot where you found Robert."

"Let's check it out." Carlita and Shelby turned onto the street and walked to the corner, past a row of boarded up buildings.

"This is it?" Shelby wrinkled her nose. "There's nothing here but a couple of abandoned buildings."

The brick buildings were close together, so close Carlita could spread her arms and touch the fronts of two of them. Almost all of the windows were boarded up. One of them had a for-sale sign nailed to the plywood. "Our next step should be to try to figure out who owns these properties. If Robert mentioned them, they must be significant."

When the women reached the corner, they climbed the small hill until they were standing on a busy thoroughfare that ran the length of the river.

They started to turn left, to head back to Walton Square when something caught Carlita's eye. "The Journey's End."

"Where?" Shelby's head whipped around.

"Over there. The news story I read mentioned Robert had been staying at a place called the Journey's End. It looks like a B&B or maybe a hostel." Carlita pointed at the two-story rambling Victorian house directly across the street.

The women waited for the light to change and let Rambo lead the way to the other side.

A white picket fence surrounded the property, giving off a warm, welcoming appearance. As they drew closer, the property showed signs of neglect.

Stray weeds sprouted between the cracks in the sidewalk. Although the exterior of the Victorian was impressive, Carlita noticed flaking paint and spots where bare wood was clearly visible. The hostel was in desperate need of a fresh coat of paint.

The women tentatively climbed the steps and approached the front door.

Shelby peered through the screen. "Hello?"

"The door is unlocked," a gruff voice replied.

Shelby pulled the screen door open and stepped inside while Carlita looped Rambo's leash around the railing. "We'll be right back." She patted his head and then followed Shelby into a dark, cramped entryway. The smell of mothballs, mixed with Pine-Sol filled the air.

"You gals looking for a place to stay?"

"No." Shelby shook her head.

"Good. Cuz we don't allow animals."

Carlita studied the thin, bearded man seated at the desk. His sharp, gray eyes met hers and crinkled in the corners as he attempted to smile. "We don't allow solicitation neither."

"We're not selling anything. Are you the proprietor?" Carlita asked.

"I'm Finch Porter. If you're asking if I own this fine establishment, then the answer is yes. Who's asking?"

"My name is Carlita Garlucci. This is my friend, Shelby. We heard Robert Towns was staying here at the Journey's End, prior to his untimely death."

"The authorities have already been here, questioning me about the man. I can't tell you much more than what I told them. The man paid cash for his room and he told me his name was

Bob Downs. He stayed here for four nights and left as quickly as he came."

Finch snapped his fingers. "One minute he was here, the next he was gone. That was a few days back. As I told the police, I don't know where he went after he left here."

"I see," Carlita said. "While Mr. Downs was staying here, did he have any visitors?"

"Nope." Finch shook his head. "Course that's not unusual and it's also not unusual for guests to pay in cash and use fake names, either."

Shelby shifted her feet. "Did Mr. Downs say or do anything that struck you as odd?"

Finch chuckled. "Young lady, nothing strikes me as odd anymore. I get all kinds of guests staying here from all over the world and each has a story. I stopped asking questions years ago. Mr. Downs kept to himself and didn't cause any trouble."

"Thank you, Mr. Finch." Carlita turned to go. "We appreciate your time."

"Wait!" Finch called out. "There is one more thing. I'm not sure what this Downs fella was up to, but this is the third time someone's been by here asking about him. First, it was the cops, then another guy and now you two."

Shelby lifted a brow. "Do you remember what the man looked like?"

"Kinda short, brown hair. He was wearing jeans and a brown shirt. I couldn't pick him out of a crowd if I tried."

"He was asking questions about Mr. Downs?" Carlita asked.

"Yep." Finch nodded. "Pretty much the exact same questions you asked."

Carlita reached into her purse and pulled out two twenty-dollar bills. "Thank you for your time, Mr. Porter." She held out the cash. "If I leave my cell phone number with you, could you please give me a call if the man who stopped by here returns?"

"You bet." Finch took the money from Carlita and shoved it into his front pocket before handing her a pen and a notepad.

She jotted her cell phone number on the pad and handed both back. "Thank you for your time."

"You're welcome."

Carlita stepped onto the porch and unwound Rambo's leash from the railing while Shelby waited for her on the sidewalk. "Do you have any idea who might have been asking about Robert?"

"No. None whatsoever." Shelby clenched her fists. "This is so frustrating. It feels like we're running in circles."

During the walk home, the women discussed the Harner Street properties and the Journey's End. Carlita wondered if the hostel and the properties Robert mentioned were somehow linked.

"We need to do a little digging around to find out who owns those properties." Carlita snapped her fingers. "Wait a minute. I know someone who might be able to help us."

She picked up the pace and Shelby hurried to keep up. "Who?"

"Remember Annie Dowton? She owns Riverfront Real Estate, right around the corner from the apartment. She might be able to help us track down the owners. Let me send her a text to see if she's around."

"I...I'm not sure that's necessary," Shelby said. "Maybe it's just an odd coincidence."

"We have so little to go on right now; I think it's worth a shot." Carlita sent Annie a text and received a quick reply that Annie was in and would be waiting for them.

When they reached Walton Square, they stopped to drop Rambo off inside the apartment and Mercedes popped out of her room. "I was beginning to wonder what happened to you. I thought you were taking Rambo to Morrell Park."

"I was and I did. I ran into Shelby along the way, so we decided to take a walk to the park where Shelby found Robert's body to have a look around."

"Did you find anything?"

"Sort of. While we were down there, Shelby remembered Robert mentioning Harner Street and the big deal he was working on. We also stopped by the Journey's End, the hostel where Robert was staying prior to his death. He was staying there under an assumed name and checked out several days ago."

Carlita explained Shelby was downstairs waiting for her and they were going to run over to Annie's real estate office to see if she could track down the owners of the Harner Street properties. "There are only a couple. I have a hunch it's not a coincidence Robert was murdered near Harner Street."

"So where did Robert go after he left the hostel?" Mercedes asked.

"I have no idea, but if we can figure that out, we might be one step closer to tracking down Robert's killer. Annie is waiting for us."

"I'll go with you." Mercedes dashed into her room and returned with her cell phone in hand. "Vinnie and Brittney left a few minutes ago to do some sightseeing."

"I'm sorry I missed them." Carlita waited for her daughter to step into the hall.

"No, you're not."

"Not what?"

"Not sorry."

Carlita paused at the top of the stairs. "Why?"

"Have you had an actual conversation with Brittney?"

"No, I mean not really."

"Let me give you a little advice. Don't," Mercedes said bluntly. "Either she's as naïve as they come or she's a talented actress."

"Mercedes," Carlita admonished. "You need to give her a fair shake. One conversation isn't enough to form an opinion."

"I suppose." Mercedes reached for the handrail. "I guess I shouldn't be so hard on her. Looking back, I was a little starry-eyed myself, before Pops died."

"And look how we've both grown." Carlita opened the alley door and joined Shelby, who was standing on the stoop. "I picked up a straggler along the way."

"Hi, Mercedes."

"Hey, Shelby. I guess that knucklehead brother of mine hasn't come to his senses yet."

"I...it's not all his fault. I'm partially to blame for not putting all of my cards on the table and letting him know what was going on with my ex." Shelby's shoulders slumped. "I'm a terrible judge of the opposite sex, dating the bad boys who always seemed to be in trouble. Tony was the first man with a clean history and past."

Mercedes snorted.

Carlita poked her in the back of the arm.

"Ouch. What was that for?" Mercedes rubbed her arm and glared at her mother.

"Try not to be so hard on yourself," Carlita said. "The street runs both ways."

Shelby's cheeks turned a tinge of pink. "Thanks for trying to help me. I still don't know if finding out who owns the Harner Street property will help."

The trio walked across the street with Carlita leading the way. She tilted her head and gazed inside the real estate office where she spotted Annie sitting at her desk.

Carlita gave her a quick wave and then opened the door. "Hey, Annie."

Annie looked up, a smile lighting her face. "Hello, ladies. What's up?"

"We need help. Actually, Shelby needs help."

"I haven't seen you in a while, Shelby. They must keep you busy working down at the post office."

"Not right now," Shelby whispered under her breath.

"I'll grab another chair." Annie popped out of her chair and hurried to her assistant, Cindy's, desk. "I see they've started on your restaurant renovations."

"Yeah. I can't wait until it's finished, not that I have time to work on it. My son, Vinnie, and his new wife are in town visiting."

Annie lifted a brow. "Oh? I didn't know Vinnie was married."

"Neither did we until yesterday. It's a long story." Carlita changed the subject. "Did you hear about the man who was murdered not far from the river?"

"Of course." Annie's head bobbed up and down. "It's all over the news."

Shelby perched on the edge of the chair Annie retrieved. "The dead man is my ex-husband, Robert, and I'm the one who found his body."

"Oh no!"

"Oh yes, and the investigators are trying to pin it on Shelby," Carlita said.

"Not only was I the one who found Robert's body, the police found a text on Robert's phone where I told him he better leave Violet and me alone or else."

"Oh dear," Annie shook her head.

"And I had some cash on me I planned to give Robert after he promised to give me the papers terminating his parental rights. I figured if I gave him what I could, he would leave Violet and me alone." Shelby's lower lip began to tremble. "The authorities found papers on Robert. They were papers he planned to file, seeking custody of Violet. He was going to trick me."

Annie pressed on the bridge of her glasses. "I don't see how the authorities can pin your ex-husband's murder on you without solid evidence."

"The reason we're here is that Shelby remembers Robert mentioning a big deal he was working on and he mentioned Harner Street. Shelby showed me the spot where she found Robert's body, and it was only steps from Harner Street," Carlita said. "We think there may be a link. That's where you come in."

"You want me to research the properties," Annie guessed.

"Yes. We hoped you might be able to search your real estate database and tell us who owns the properties. There are only a couple of buildings. One is for sale and the rest are vacant, at least as far as we can tell."

"Of course I can." Annie's fingers hovered over the keyboard. "You can also find the owner's name on the Board of Assessor's website." She tapped the keys. "One of the properties is owned by the City of Savannah, seized for non-payment of taxes."

Annie's brow furrowed as she studied the screen. "Actually, there are two properties owned by the city. Judging by the information here, it appears they're empty."

"That makes sense. They looked empty," Carlita said.

"There's one more property." Annie grew quiet. "Four twelve Harner Street. A deed was recently recorded. It lists East Coast Ventures, LLC as the owner."

"Does it give the owners' names?" Carlita asked.

"No. Unfortunately, it does not. If they formed the company a short time ago, the information might not be available online yet. We can still check," Annie said.

"If it's not too much trouble," Carlita said.

"Of course not." Annie turned her attention back to her keyboard and the women sat quietly listening to her fingernails tapping the keys. "There is a record of an East Coast Ventures, but no other information is currently available."

Carlita stood. "So we're back to square one."

Annie walked the women to the door. "I'm sorry I couldn't get you the information. If you think of anything else, give me a call."

Carlita thanked Annie, and then followed her daughter and Shelby out of the office and back to their apartment building.

When they reached the back door, they discovered the door ajar. "Mercedes, you were the last one out. Did you forget to pull the door shut?"

Mercedes shook her head. "I don't think so. Although you know how it sometimes sticks. Maybe Vinnie and Brittney came back and didn't shut the door all of the way."

"Huh." Carlita pulled the door shut and gave it a hard push. "I need to remind them to check the door to make sure it's shut." She turned to Shelby. "Is now a good time for Tony and you to have a chat?"

"Yes. I'd like to run upstairs and freshen up first."

"Of course." Carlita waited until Mercedes and Shelby reached the top of the stairs before opening the pawnshop's back door. She was halfway inside when a woman's bloodcurdling scream stopped her dead in her tracks.

Chapter 11

Tony heard the scream too, bolted out the back door, past Carlita and ran up the stairs.

Carlita was hot on his heels as she raced up the steps where Mercedes and Shelby stood in Shelby's doorway.

"What's going on?" Tony grasped both of Shelby's arms. "Are you okay?"

"Yes," she whispered. "My apartment..."

Carlita barreled past her daughter and tenant, and followed her son into Shelby's apartment. She stopped short, taking a quick gasp of air at the sight of Shelby's home.

The couch cushions were torn off, the living room curtains lay in a heap on the floor, the table lamp was broken, the lampshade punctured. The kitchen was in a similar sad state of disrepair. All of the cabinets were wide open, the contents strewn along the counter and on the floor.

The bathroom medicine cabinet was open, but not nearly as messy as the bedrooms, which were in the same condition as the main part of the apartment.

Tony's eyes sparked with anger. "What I wanna know is how someone got in here."

"I don't know, son. Violet left with Shelby's aunt and uncle. Shelby, Mercedes and I were over at Annie's office. When we returned, we found the back door ajar. Mercedes thinks she closed it, but isn't certain. Did you hear anything?"

"Nope. The store has been busy, with people in and out all day. Did you notice if someone busted down the door?"

"I didn't." Carlita followed Tony to the living room and the front door.

Tony leaned in for a closer inspection of the door and lock. "There's no sign of forced entry."

He nodded at Shelby, who was still standing in the hall. "Did you lock this on your way out?"

"I...I think so. I mean, I'm usually careful about locking the door." She pressed a hand to her forehead. "With the way the last couple of days have gone, my head isn't on straight. There's a chance I left the door unlocked."

"Either way, someone tore your place apart. Do you have any idea what they were looking for?"

Shelby's eyes grew round as saucers and she shook her head. "I have no idea, but I've been getting the feeling that someone is following me. This has something to do with Robert's death, or whoever was after him."

"And now they're after something." Tony stared at the door thoughtfully. "It's not safe for you to stay here Shelby. We need to call the authorities and report the break-in."

"I...don't want anyone in the apartment right now, plus I need to leave soon to head to my aunt and uncle's house." Shelby gave Carlita a helpless look.

"C'mon Mercedes." Carlita motioned to her daughter. "Let's you and I go inside and see if we can straighten the place up."

Carlita patted her son on the shoulder. "I think it's time for you and Shelby to talk." She reached into her front pocket and handed her son the keys to her apartment. "You can talk in my place. What about the store?"

"I got one of my part-timers covering. Could you let them know I'll be back down in a minute?"

"I will." Carlita waited for Tony and Shelby to step inside her apartment before she hurried down the stairs.

She pulled the store employee off to the side and explained to her that Tony was taking care of an urgent matter and would be down shortly.

The employee assured Carlita she could handle the store until he returned, so Carlita made her way back to Shelby's apartment where Mercedes was in the process of cleaning the kitchen. "Someone did a real number on this place."

"They sure did." Carlita shook her head in disgust. "As if Shelby doesn't already have enough on her plate, now she's gotta worry about this."

"Are Tony and Shelby still talking?"

"Yeah. I hope they can patch things up." Carlita picked up a sofa cushion and tucked it back in place. "The poor thing needs all of us on her side."

"What if..." Mercedes' voice trailed off.

Carlita reached for another cushion. "What if what?"

"I dunno." Mercedes shrugged. "Never mind."

"No." Carlita made her way into the kitchen. "What were you going to say?"

"I was gonna say, what if Shelby was involved in her ex's death." Mercedes hurried on. "We don't know her that well. I mean, think about it. We didn't even know she had family in the area and poof! Next thing you know, they're here. Then there's the fact that she didn't want to report the break-in. I don't understand."

"She was avoiding her family because of Robert."

"What if Shelby did this to make it look like someone was after her?"

"You write too many crime stories," Carlita joked. "Seriously, I've got a gut for bad apples and Shelby is not a bad person. I would almost bet money she isn't capable of murdering her ex-husband."

"Even if the ex-husband threatened to take Violet away and she felt she had no other choice? Shelby found his body. She also admitted she sent him a threatening text. Perhaps this was her opportunity to get rid of Robert once and for all, and make it look like someone else did the deed."

"That's a stretch," Carlita argued. "Remember, Shelby is already the prime suspect."

"I think it was convenient we just so happened to all be gone when this took place. Tony never heard a thing, the back door was ajar and there was no sign of forced entry."

Before Carlita could answer, the apartment door opened and a pale Shelby crept inside.

Carlita hurried to her side. "How did it go?"

"Okay." Shelby's hand trembled as she handed Carlita her house keys. "We called a truce and agreed we had more important things to worry about than whose feelings got hurt."

"That's a start," Carlita patted her arm. "Why don't you go to the bedroom and pack some things to take to your uncle's house and we'll keep working on getting this place back in order?"

"Okay."

Mother and daughter worked fast to clean up the mess. By the time Shelby emerged from the bedroom, the apartment showed little signs of the previous state of disarray.

"Thanks for cleaning up. I'll never be able to repay you for all that you've done for Violet and me. I do have one more favor to ask." Shelby rolled her suitcase off to the side. "I was wondering if I could hitch a ride to my uncle's place."

"Ma and I can drop you off," Mercedes said. "I'll go grab the car keys."

Carlita waited in the hall while Shelby locked her apartment door and Mercedes dashed in the apartment to grab the keys.

When they reached the alley, Carlita got the distinct feeling they were being watched. She waited until Mercedes and Shelby were in the car and the doors were locked. "Remind me to stop by Elvira's place later to see if she noticed anything suspicious."

Mercedes reached for her seatbelt. "That's a great idea, Ma. Maybe Elvira caught someone on camera, sneaking in the back door. What's your uncle's address Shelby? I'll put it in the GPS."

Shelby rattled off the address.

"Thanks." Mercedes began humming and abruptly stopped. "Oh!"

Carlita jumped, tightening her grip on the steering wheel. "You scared me half to death."

"Sorry, Ma. I was gonna say, Vinnie said he had something to take care of first thing tomorrow morning and asked me if I would take Brittney to the mall. She wants to go shoe shopping."

"Have fun," Carlita said.

"I was hoping you would go with us."

"Shoe shopping? You know I'm not big on shopping."

"C'mon," Mercedes pleaded. "You gotta go. It will be a bonding experience. Remember, you're the one who said I had to give Brittney a chance. This way, we'll both get to know her better."

"You're using my own words against me." Carlita cast her daughter a quick glance. "All right. How about maybe?"

Shelby was unusually quiet in the back seat of the car. Carlita glanced in the rearview mirror. "Are you okay Shelby? You seem awfully quiet."

"I was thinking about the Harner Street property, how close it was to the Journey's End, not to mention the spot where Robert was shot. It seems like the three are somehow connected. Then I remembered how he wanted me to meet him at the Black Stallion Club."

"We can gauge the distance using the GPS." Mercedes leaned forward in her seat. "I'll pull up a map of the riverfront area. Harner Street is our first destination and the Black Stallion Club is our next destination." She grew silent as she worked on the GPS. "Shelby, you might be onto something."

"It's close, isn't it?"

"Yes, it's only a couple of blocks away from Harner Street." Mercedes squinted her eyes and studied the screen. "Those four locations...the Black Stallion Club, Harner Street, the park where Shelby found Robert's body and the Journey's End form a square. One could easily walk to all four of them within a few minutes."

Shelby cleared her throat. "I think I just remembered something else."

Chapter 12

"Really?" Carlita tightened her grip on the steering wheel. "What is it that you remembered?"

"The name Pat. Robert mentioned the name Pat."

Mercedes shifted in the seat. "Did you ask him who Pat was?"

"No. I mean, looking back I should have. At the time, my only concern was to get rid of Robert once and for all."

"We're getting close," Carlita turned off the main road, onto a secondary road. They drove for another mile and then turned onto a dirt drive. The car bounced along the rutted path. "This place is in the middle of nowhere."

"My aunt and uncle like their privacy."

"No kidding." Carlita crept along the drive until they reached a clearing and a sprawling brick ranch.

"This is it."

Carlita steered the car along the circle drive and stopped in front of the garage. "Would you like us to wait to make sure they're home?"

"If you don't mind." Shelby flung the door open, got out and then reached back inside for her suitcase. "Thanks for giving me a ride." She dragged her suitcase up the drive and past the garage before disappearing around the corner.

She emerged moments later and gave Carlita a thumbs-up and a wave.

Mercedes waited until she was out of sight. "There's something fishy going on, Ma. Shelby's reaction makes me think maybe we're not getting the whole story from her. Maybe she's still in shock and slowly remembering details or maybe not."

"Are you still thinking she may have had something to do with her ex's death?"

"I don't know what to think," Mercedes said. "So now what?"

"I know I swore I didn't want to involve Elvira, but her exterior surveillance cameras may be able to give us some clues as to who broke into Shelby's apartment and ransacked the place."

Carlita continued. "There was something else. The owner of the Journey's End told us not only had the police questioned him, another man stopped by to ask questions about Robert."

"Did he give you any indication who the person was?"

"No. He gave us a description. He said the man was kinda short, with brown hair. He was wearing jeans and a brown shirt. I gave him forty bucks and my cell phone number, and asked him to give me a call if the man came back."

"That was smart thinkin', Ma."

"I come up with a good idea every once in a while," Carlita joked.

When they arrived back home, Vinnie's car was still gone.

Carlita stopped by the pawnshop to let Tony know Shelby was at her uncle's house and they were going to run by Elvira's place to see if she'd seen or heard anything around the time of the break-in.

No one answered Elvira's door, so the two women circled around the front to the business entrance. The doors were locked and the lights were off.

Carlita peered through the front window. "That's odd."

"Maybe they're all on assignment," Mercedes joked.

"You would think Elvira would have someone here to keep the office open. I'll send her a text."

Carlita reached into her purse and pulled out her cell phone. She tapped a quick message and then hit the send button. "I guess we'll have to wait."

"I think I'll do a little research on the riverfront district before I tackle my new book draft."

The women circled the block before returning to the apartment. Carlita followed Mercedes to her room. "Are you still working on your second mafia series book?"

"Yeah, and I'm bogged down in the middle. There are too many victims and not enough suspects. I need to head back to New York to dig up some really gritty stuff."

"All you gotta do is interview your brother, Vinnie. I'm sure he has plenty of stories that involve the family," Carlita said.

Mercedes plopped down in her chair. "Now that you mention it, Brittney did give me some ideas for a new character for the book. I could fashion the killer's personality after her, seeing how she seems so innocent. In reality, she's a cold, calculating serial killer, working for her daddy, the kingpin mobster. She dates men her dad wants taken out and then she does the deed."

"Maybe that's where you're coming up with the idea somehow Shelby is involved in her ex's murder," Carlita mused.

"No." Mercedes shook her head. "Shelby's situation is different. Something isn't adding up. I mean, why wouldn't Shelby report her ex to the authorities instead of agreeing to meet him all alone? And why was she going to give him money? It would only encourage him to hang around and keep hounding her for more, even if he did agree to sign away his parental rights."

Carlita wandered to Mercedes' bedroom window, lifted the blinds and peered out into the courtyard. "You have some valid points."

Mercedes reached for her mouse. "I hate to say it, but Shelby *is* a suspect and I think she's headed to the slammer. Until I have a clear direction for my mafia story, I was thinking about moving on to heavier stuff, maybe something along the lines of a psychological thriller."

"And mafia murders aren't heavy enough?"

"You know what I mean. I want something grittier, a glued to the edge of your seat with your armpits sweating and looking over your shoulder because you're sure a slasher is about to take you out story."

"It's a wonder you can sleep at night, Mercedes. I see Bob Lowman's truck parked out front. I'm going to run downstairs to check on the restaurant's progress."

Mercedes had already turned her attention to her laptop, her fingers flying over the keyboard, so her mother tiptoed out of the room, quietly closing the door behind her.

She swung by the pawnshop to check on Tony and ask if he needed help. There was only one shopper, who was browsing the electronics aisle, so Carlita slipped out of the store and made her way to her other property.

The sound of hammers pounding drifted from the front entrance and she took a tentative step inside. Drywall sheets covered the walls of what would be the front reception area as well as the main dining room.

Carlita steered clear of the workers and carefully stepped over the equipment as she searched for Bob, the owner of the construction company. She found him in the kitchen, frowning at some pipes.

"I don't like the look on your face," Carlita said.

"Hi, Carlita." Bob gave her a quick smile and jabbed a finger at the ceiling. "It looks like we're going to have to tear out these pipes. There's no way they'll pass the next building inspection."

"Great. How much will replacing them set me back?"

"I already figured in the expense based on the age of the building. Although I hesitate to call this place a money pit, it's been neglected for many years and needs some major updates."

Carlita patted Bob's arm. "I understand. Believe me, after what we went through renovating the apartments and the pawnshop, I knew what we were getting into with this project."

"Would you like to take a look at what we've done since the last time you stopped by?"

"Yes," Carlita nodded. "I took a look around the other night after the workers left. I'm impressed with the progress."

Bob and Carlita walked around the property while Bob showed her the work he and his men had done. They finished the tour near the back of the building and in front of what would be the public restrooms.

"Before you go, I wanted to mention there was some guy in here earlier. He was asking a bunch of questions. He wanted to know who owned this property and did I know anything about an apartment unit for rent."

Carlita nodded. "I ran an ad in the local paper, trying to find a new tenant. If anyone stops to ask again, the unit is rented. What did he look like?"

"He was about five six, brown hair. He seemed nervous."

A cold chill ran down Carlita's spine as she thought about the mystery man who was asking questions at the Journey's End. "He didn't happen to mention his name, did he?"

"Nope." Bob shook his head. "Like I said, he appeared a little edgy, asked a couple of questions and then took off."

"If he shows up again, can you give me a call?"

"Will do."

Carlita turned to go and then turned back. "Have you ever heard of Savannah Sam? He's my new tenant."

"You must be talking about Sam Ivey. He's well-known around here and one of the more popular local tour guides. Sam is a former cop. He quit the force a few years back and decided to start his own tour guide operation. He offers historic walking tours by day and ghost tours at night."

Carlita's eyes widened. "Did you say Sam Ivey is a former cop?"

"Yes," Bob nodded. "He was a county cop."

"Hey, Bob. You got a minute?" One of the construction crew began walking toward them.

"I better let you get back to work. Thanks for the update and for letting me know about the stranger who stopped by."

"You're welcome." Bob promised to give her a call if the man appeared again.

Carlita waved good-bye and then slipped out the back door. She made it as far as her back door when she heard someone call her name.

Elvira was standing in her doorway, waving frantically. "Hey. I got your message."

Carlita slowly walked across the alley. "I..."

Elvira lifted a hand to cut her off. "Before you say anything else, I wanted to let you know I think I may have a break in the murder case."

Chapter 13

"What case?"

Carlita followed Elvira into her building.

"The Robert Towns' murder case. I started doing a little digging around into Towns' background. The man was bad news and had a lengthy criminal record."

Elvira shut the door behind them. "It goes back at least a decade. Makes me wonder how a woman like Shelby could get tangled up with a guy like him."

"What kind of criminal record?"

"It started out with petty theft, drug possession. Last year he was arrested for armed robbery. Got off on a technicality or a corrupt judge, take your pick. The charges were dropped and he was back on the streets."

Elvira snatched her cell phone off the counter. "There's been nothing for the last year, after the armed robbery incident."

"So maybe he decided to go clean," Carlita said.

"I doubt it. If so, why did someone murder him? After finishing my research and reading the news story about his death, how Shelby found his body in a park, not far from the riverfront district, I said to myself, 'Elvira, you need to head over to the riverfront area and have a look around.'"

"I can save you a trip," Carlita said. "Shelby and I were already there. There's nothing to see except a small park and some empty buildings."

"Huh." Elvira lifted her brow. "I may have underestimated your investigative techniques after all."

"I'll take that as a compliment."

"So, back to my story. I was on my way out the back door when I happened to notice a lurker hanging around in the alley. At first, I thought it was your son, Vinnie. When I took a closer look, I realized it wasn't him."

"Do you know who it was?"

"Nope." Elvira shook her head. "Never seen him before in my life. He was acting kinda funny, as if he was casing the joint. Check it out."

Elvira switched her phone on, clicked the camera icon and then handed it to Carlita. "I wasn't able to get a real clear picture of the guy cuz I didn't want him to see me. I checked my surveillance camera and he was just out of the visual range, which reminds me, I need to tweak my cameras for a better visual on the back of your building."

"I'm sure," Carlita frowned. She studied the photo of the man with light brown hair. Was this the stranger who stopped by the Journey's End? Could he be the man with brown hair that Bob

Lowman mentioned or possibly even the person who ransacked Shelby's apartment?

"Do you recognize him?" Elvira asked.

"No, but then it's impossible to recognize someone when the only thing you have to go on is the back of their head."

Elvira ignored the comment and swiped the screen. "He was acting suspicious, so I followed him."

"Where did he go?"

"To the Black Stallion. Here's another shot of the man going into the club. He stopped to talk to someone near the front door before going in."

Carlita squinted her eyes and studied the photo of the man. This time it was a side shot. "How is this a clue?"

"It's all about the body language. Did I ever mention I studied body language? Anyhoo, I could tell by the expressions on their faces they were having a serious conversation. The man I was following, let's call him Carmine...Carmine was walking into the Black Stallion, said something to a person I believe may have been a bouncer. There was a brief exchange. Carmine said something the bouncer didn't like, he grabbed Carmine's arm to stop him. Carmine jerked his arm away and stormed into the establishment."

Carlita handed the phone back. "I've never seen this man before in my life. I've never been inside the Black Stallion and I don't recognize the bouncer outside the club. Someone broke into Shelby's apartment around the same time you saw this person lurking about."

"You're serious?"

"Yes. They ransacked her place."

"Well." Elvira cleared her throat. "Far be it from me to tell you that you keep questionable company, or at the very least your children do. I would definitely be on guard until we figure out who the mystery man is, and who killed Shelby's ex."

Elvira snapped her fingers. "Wait a minute. Are you sure this wasn't a love triangle gone bad?"

"What are you talking about?"

"A crime of passion." Elvira began to pace. "Perhaps Shelby was carrying on with her ex, right under Tony's nose. He found out and then snuffed him out."

"That's absurd," Carlita sputtered. "You're talking about my son. He's not capable of committing murder." *At least Carlita didn't think he was capable of murder.*

"It still doesn't explain the mystery man lurking about or who may have trashed Shelby's apartment."

Elvira abruptly stopped. "It's obvious what our next logical step should be."

"What do you mean 'our next step?' This matter doesn't involve you."

"It most certainly does involve me. We share common areas and I don't like the idea of questionable characters lurking about, breaking into people's homes."

"That's a lame excuse."

"Lame or not, I've already invested time in the investigation and I plan to proceed with the next step."

"Which is?" Carlita asked, although she wasn't sure she would like the answer.

"I think it's time for us to pay a visit to the Black Stallion Club."

Carlita chewed her lower lip and studied Elvira. The woman was right. Somehow, the club was linked to Robert. "I need to handle a couple of small matters before we head down there. Can you hold off until later?"

"Later tonight?"

"I'm not sure. I have some other matters to handle first."

"Okay. Keep in mind time is of the essence. There's not much action in the district during the day. Nighttime would be a better time to conduct an undercover/covert surveillance mission."

******

After Carlita left Elvira's place, she headed to the pawnshop. Tony and the part-timer, Melody, were both working. She made a beeline for her son. "I need your help."

"Sure, Ma." Tony, noting the tone of his mother's voice, gave her his full attention. "What's up?"

"There's a property in the riverfront area I want to scope out."

"So? Go scope it out," Tony said.

"No, I mean scope out the inside."

"You want to break in?"

"If that's what it takes," Carlita said bluntly. "There's a property on Harner Street, a property which was recently purchased by a private group. I think it's linked to Shelby's ex and I want to take a look at it while Shelby's not around."

Tony rubbed the stubble on his chin. "You think Shelby might be involved in her ex's death?"

"I don't know what to think, son. What I do know is the Journey's End, the hostel where Robert was staying prior to his death, the Black Stallion Club, the spot where Shelby found Robert's body and this property on Harner Street are all within striking distance of each other. Shelby and I already talked to the owner of the Journey's End. Robert checked out of the hostel several days before his death. Where did he go?"

"So you think maybe he was hanging out in a vacant property near the river?" Tony asked.

"Maybe."

"Okay, I'll go with you. Is Mercedes going, too?"

"It wouldn't hurt to have her tag along. She's good at catching clues."

"Let me talk to Melody. I'll meet you and Mercedes in the alley in ten minutes."

Carlita thanked her son and climbed the steps to the apartment. "Mercedes? You in here?"

"Yeah, Ma." Mercedes emerged from her room. "How's the reno?"

"It's great." Carlita briefly told her daughter about her conversation with Bob Lowman, the strange man who stopped by to ask questions and how Elvira spotted what appeared to be the same man lurking about. "She took a picture of him before following him to the Black Stallion Club. He fits the description of the guy nosing around at Journey's End."

Carlita grabbed her keys off the hook. "I asked Tony to go to Harner Street with me. I want to take a closer look at the vacant property while Shelby isn't around."

"You want me to go with you?"

"I thought you'd never ask. I'm meeting Tony downstairs in a few minutes."

"Let me grab some stuff." Mercedes darted into her room and joined her mother moments later. "I'm good to go."

"You got your gun?"

Mercedes patted her jacket pocket. "Of course. You never know what we're going to run into when we get there."

Chapter 14

Tony offered to drive to Harner Street. Carlita quickly agreed, since she'd already walked the entire river area earlier and her feet were sore. She also figured they might need to make a quick getaway, depending on what they found.

When they reached the riverfront, Tony drove around the block, then around the Journey's End before making a U-turn and heading back to Harner Street. "You're right Ma. These places are all within a few short blocks. You may be onto something."

Tony parked the car in the public parking lot adjacent to Harner Street. Their first stop was the park where Shelby found Robert's body.

She pointed to the other side of the street. "This is what got me to thinking. Do you see how close this property is to where Shelby found Robert's body?"

The trio crossed the street to the other side.

"We're looking for 412 Harner Street."

Tony studied the buildings. "What about the other ones?"

"According to Annie, the city owns the other properties after seizing them for non-payment of taxes. Four-twelve Harner was recently purchased by a group called East Coast Ventures."

"Who owns it?" Tony asked.

"Annie couldn't tell. The property transfer happened recently and the owner records haven't been updated yet. This is it." Carlita stopped abruptly. "I see a courtyard between the buildings."

Carlita stepped over to the gate. It creaked loudly when she pushed it open. She took a tentative step inside, with Tony right behind her.

"Hang on Ma." He pulled a gun from his front pocket and eased past his mother, leading the way into the courtyard.

Thick, green ivy covered the concrete walls and crept up the sides to a small, square window.

Carlita was so focused on the exterior of the building; she didn't notice the uneven cobblestones and tripped on one of them.

Tony reached out to steady her. "You better watch where you're going."

"Sorry," Carlita whispered.

Loose pebbles crunched under their feet and the sound echoed against the walls of the neglected courtyard. The area reminded Carlita of what her courtyard had looked like the first time she'd laid eyes on it.

They stopped near the center and Carlita spun in a slow circle, her sharp eye taking in the mold tinted center fountain. Next to the fountain was a pile of shattered terra cotta pots. In front of the broken pots was a pair of rusty wrought iron benches that faced each other.

"Over here." Carlita motioned to a window and pair of black shutters. "These shutters aren't latched."

Mercedes stood off to the side, near the door while Tony tugged on the edge of one of the shutters. It swung open.

"You see that?"

"See what?"

"The shutter didn't squeak. If this building was abandoned, the shutters would be nailed shut to keep people out." Tony swung the other shutter open before tucking his gun in the waistband of his pants and grasping the window sash. The window was locked.

Mercedes twisted the knob on the door. "This is locked, too. Where is Autumn when you need her?"

"Let me try." Tony stepped to the door and wiggled the loose knob. "Stand back." He twisted the knob hard and the lock popped. "These old locks are a piece of cake to open."

Tony stepped inside the building, Mercedes followed her brother and Carlita brought up the rear. To the right of the entrance was a wide-open space. To the left was a row of doors.

Tony reached for the nearest knob. He pushed the door open and peered inside. "It's a closet."

Tony shut the door and opened the door next to it. "Bathroom. Nasty at that." He closed the door and made his way to the third and final door. "Lucky door number three. There's something in here."

Carlita hovered in the doorway and watched as he crossed the room and knelt next to a small cooler.

Mercedes joined her brother. "I wonder what's in here." She lifted the lid and the stench of rotting food blasted her in the face. She started to gag and pinched her nose. "There's a bottled water and something gross in there."

"It looks like it's been here a coupla days." Tony touched the small ice pack that was inside the cooler. "The ice pack is warm."

Carlita jumped at a small scuttling noise and darted into the room. "This place is giving me the creeps. Stop playing with the food and let's go."

"There's nothing in here." Tony stood. "Other than the cooler, the place is clean."

Carlita turned to go when her foot caught on something and she stumbled. "I keep tripping over my own feet."

"No, Ma." Mercedes shook her head. "There's something sticking up."

"It's a ring." Tony grasped the ring and gave it a sharp tug. A rectangular piece of the flooring popped up, revealing a trapdoor. "Stand back."

Tony leaned forward for a closer inspection. On one end was a metal ladder leading down to murky darkness.

"Hand me your phone."

Mercedes handed her phone to him. He turned the flashlight on and shined the light into the opening. "There's something down there. I'm gonna check it out."

"Be careful son." Carlita and Mercedes hovered near the opening while Tony descended the steps, the light from Mercedes' phone bouncing off the floor.

There was a momentary silence and then Tony's voice echoed up. "I think I got something."

Carlita listened to the *thunk* of Tony's steps on the ladder and he re-emerged holding a black backpack. He slid it onto the wooden floor next to his mother. "There are a coupla tunnels down here. One looks like it leads to the river, but it's blocked off. There's another one that's open and I wanna see where it goes."

"I'll go with you." Mercedes scrambled to the edge of the ladder. "Ma, you stay here and keep a look out."

"I don't like this," Carlita eyed the opening. "You don't know what you're gonna run into."

Tony patted his pocket. "I got my glock."

Mercedes pulled her small pistol from her pocket and handed it to her mother. "Hang onto this."

Carlita took the gun. "Please be careful."

Mercedes scampered down the ladder and joined Tony, who was shining the light around the dark, dank space. "See that tunnel? I think it leads to the river. There's another one over here." He shifted the phone to his other hand and eased his gun out of his pocket. "Stay close."

"You won't have to worry about that." Mercedes stepped next to her brother and they slowly inched their way along the narrow tunnel. Except for the shuffling of their feet and an occasional dripping sound, the tunnel was eerily quiet.

"I think we're walking along the river," Mercedes whispered.

The tunnel continued for what seemed like forever and abruptly ended in front of a brick wall and another metal ladder. Tony handed his sister his gun and stuck his foot on the bottom rung.

"What are you doing?" Mercedes hissed.

"Checkin' it out. Keep the gun handy."

"I think this is a bad idea."

Tony ignored his sister and crept up the steps. At the top was a wooden trapdoor. He shoved Mercedes' cell phone in his pocket and tightened his grip on the ladder. Using his free hand, he pushed on the trapdoor. It didn't budge.

He tried again and it refused to give way.

Tony descended the steps and joined his sister at the bottom. "It's locked on the other side."

"I have an idea." Mercedes held out the gun. "I'll trade you. Hand me my phone and take your gun."

The two switched and Mercedes tapped the front of her cell phone.

"What are you doing?"

"I have an app on my phone that counts steps. I'm going to count the number of steps we take to get back to Ma. We know the direction we're walking. All we gotta do is walk the same number of steps along the river and Voila! We'll be able to figure out where this tunnel ends."

"That's a good idea Mercedes."

"I'm full of good ideas."

The siblings retraced their steps, returning to the open trapdoor.

Mercedes climbed up the steps first and joined her mother. Tony followed his sister out of the tunnel and then slid the trapdoor back in place.

"What did you find?" Carlita handed the backpack to her son and returned Mercedes' gun to her.

"There's a tunnel leading to the river. The tunnel is blocked. There's a second tunnel. It dead ends at another ladder and trapdoor, but it was locked on the other side."

"So you don't know where it goes?"

"Nope, but Mercedes has an idea."

"A brilliant idea," Mercedes interrupted.

"Yes, Mercedes has a *brilliant* idea and we're gonna check it out just as soon as we find out what's in the backpack."

The trio exited the building and Tony closed the door behind them. He followed his mother and sister into the courtyard before he set the backpack on the ground and unzipped the front compartment. The pocket was empty.

He opened the second one. Inside the compartment were a handheld calculator, two ink pens, and a yellow pad with handwritten notes. Tony squinted his eyes and studied the notes. "This looks like Greek to me." He dropped the items back into the compartment and unzipped the large, center compartment where he pulled out a laptop.

Tony flipped it open. "It has battery left, but there's a password lock."

"Rats," Mercedes said.

"We'll have to see if we can figure out how to bypass the password." Tony closed the lid and slid the laptop back inside. "There's something else in here."

Tony stuck his hand inside and pulled out a bulky manila envelope. "What's this?" He tipped the envelope over and dumped the contents onto the ground. "Whoa. Check this out!"

Chapter 15

Several thick stacks of hundred dollar bills fell to the ground and he began counting the cash. "There's over a hundred thousand dollars here."

"Robert," Carlita said. "I bet a million bucks this backpack belonged to Robert. Why would he tell Shelby he needed money if he had all of this?"

"Because the man was a sick, twisted individual who wanted his ex-wife and child to be penniless. We're gonna take it with us." Tony shoved the cash inside the envelope and the envelope inside the backpack before zipping it shut. "We need to have Shelby take a look at the handwritten notes. She should be able to tell if the writing belongs to her ex."

Tony slung the backpack over his shoulder and stood. "Let's get outta here."

He strode out of the courtyard and Carlita and Mercedes hurried to keep up. "We're gonna tell Shelby we broke into the building?"

"Why not? She should be relieved we're onto something."

"True," Carlita said.

Tony waited for his mother and sister to exit the courtyard before pulling the gate shut. "If this backpack belonged to Robert, it definitely gives someone another reason to take him out."

"Hang on a sec. Let me start testing my walking app." Mercedes tapped the cell phone screen. "We need to add a couple of feet since we're already out of the building, but this should get us close."

The trio walked in a straight line, down the sidewalk that ran adjacent to the river, past the few remaining buildings on Harner Street. They crossed onto a side street and reached an area bustling with businesses.

They crossed one more intersection and Mercedes held up a hand. "This is it." She stopped to inspect the back of the building. "What is it?"

"It's the back of a building, Sis."

"No kidding," Mercedes snapped. "We need to figure out what it is." She took a step back and counted the buildings. "It's the third one in. Let's circle around to the other side."

They continued to the next corner, turned right and walked to the other end of the block. It spilled onto a main thoroughfare.

"We're almost there," Mercedes said. "It's the next building.

When they reached the building, Carlita's breath caught in her throat. "It's the Black Stallion Club."

"It makes perfect sense," Mercedes said. "Now all we gotta do is confirm who the backpack belongs to."

The trio returned to Tony's car and he waited until they were safely inside and the doors locked before speaking. "I say we keep this to ourselves until I can unlock the computer and find out what's on it."

"Agreed," Carlita and Mercedes said in unison.

It was a quick drive back to Walton Square. Tony pulled into an empty spot and they exited the car.

Elvira must've been watching for Mercedes and Carlita to return because she was waiting for them in the alley. "Did you take care of your pressing business?"

"To some degree," Carlita said evasively.

"We still need to hammer out our plans."

"Plans for what?" Tony asked.

"We're going to hang out," Elvira said.

"Huh. Right. I'm gonna head inside and put this in a safe place." Tony shrugged off the backpack and turned to his mother. "I'll be in the pawnshop if you need me." He walked into the building and gave the trio one final look before quietly closing the door.

Elvira waited until the door was shut. "I was thinking about something. You still have an inkling of suspicion Shelby hasn't told you everything?"

"Yes," Carlita admitted. "I do."

"You have a key to her apartment. Now is the golden opportunity to search it."

"Search her apartment," Mercedes wrinkled her nose. "Without her permission?"

"You have her permission. If my memory serves me correctly, there's a section somewhere in your ironclad rental agreement where Shelby gave you permission to enter her apartment even if she's not present."

"That's a gray area," Carlita said.

"It is? You broke into my apartment when I wasn't home. You also brought your buddies with you to search my place."

"You were missing, Elvira. Not only were you missing, you ended up getting kidnapped."

"And we saved your life," Mercedes chimed in. "If Ma hadn't been concerned about your safety, you would be dead by now."

"I would've figured out a way to escape the evil clutches of that madman," Elvira scoffed.

"You're making light of a serious situation," Carlita said.

"You don't think this is serious, too? A man has been murdered and there's a chance you might be harboring a killer."

Carlita sucked in a breath and briefly closed her eyes. Once again, Elvira was right. The evidence pointed to Shelby somehow being involved in her ex's murder, and even if she wasn't, at the very least, she suspected her tenant was hiding something.

"I hate to admit it, Ma, but Elvira is right. Something fishy is going on and Shelby is not being completely honest with us. People commit crimes of passion all of the time. We both know the lengths she went to, to hide from her ex-husband, how freaked out she was by the thought he might take Violet from her," Mercedes said.

Elvira patted Carlita's arm. "If you don't have the stomach for it, I'll volunteer to do the deed myself. I have no qualms about searching Shelby's apartment."

"I'm sure you don't," Carlita said wryly. "No. I'm the landlord. It's my responsibility to ensure the safety and security of my tenants. I don't want to tip Tony off, at least not yet. If he suspects Shelby is withholding something else from him, their relationship is toast and I'll be the one to take the blame."

"It could be a blessing in disguise," Elvira said. "I figure I'm a good judge of character, but even I have to admit if Shelby is involved in some criminal activity and the death of her ex, she has me fooled."

Carlita glanced at her watch. "Daylight is burning. I would like to get this over with as quickly as possible."

"I think you're making a wise decision in searching her place now. You can't let the trail go cold. You have to strike while the iron is hot. Are you sure you don't need a hand?" Elvira asked eagerly. "I could be your lookout and guard the alley in case Shelby shows up."

"No," Carlita shook her head. "It won't be necessary. I appreciate you letting me know about the mystery man earlier."

"My surveillance cameras have come in *mighty* handy if I do say so myself."

"Yes, they have."

Elvira looked disappointed as Mercedes and Carlita stepped into their building.

"Are you sure you wanna snoop inside Shelby's place, Ma?"

"I don't, but I also don't see where we have a choice."

Mercedes waited in the upper hall while Carlita dashed into their apartment to retrieve her set of master keys.

"There you are." Vinnie emerged from their temporary abode at the same time his mother stepped into the hall with the keys. "We wondered what happened to you."

"Mercedes and I had to take care of something." Carlita quickly changed the subject. "How was your morning of sightseeing?"

"Eh." Vinnie shrugged. "I'm not much into seein' the sights. Brittney enjoyed it. We took the trolley tour and a ride on the paddleboat. That was cool. We grabbed a bite to eat in the City

194

Market district and then did a little shopping before heading back."

Vinnie nodded to his sister. "You still gonna take Brittney shoe shopping in the morning? I got a little business to take care of and figured while you girls are maxing out my plastic, I could take care of my stuff."

"Yes, I'll take Brittney shoe shopping in the morning," Mercedes said. "If I remember correctly, the new mall has several designer shoe stores. Brittney should have a field day."

"Thanks, Mercedes. I owe you one. I guess now that I've given Savannah a chance, it's not such a bad place to visit," Vinnie said.

"It's also a great place to live. You should consider it if you get tired of Atlantic City," Carlita hinted.

"Not a chance. This place is nice enough, although a little too low key for my tastes. Speaking of tastes, Brittney and I would like to treat the family to dinner tonight."

"That would be nice," Carlita said. "Have you asked Tony?"

"Yeah, we just came from there. He told me he had a few things to take care of after work, but said he could be ready by seven-thirty. We're gonna meet downstairs near the back door."

"Seven-thirty is perfect. It will give Mercedes and me time to take care of a couple of things ourselves. Do you have a restaurant in mind?"

"Brittney spotted a tapas restaurant she wants to try, if you don't mind."

"Tapas?" Carlita lifted a brow.

"You know, those cutesy little food dishes people share at the table. I wouldn't mind checkin' it out since we're thinking of closing one of the bakery restaurants in the casino and opening something new and fresh. According to Brittney, tapas are all the rage."

"I'm game. Tapas sounds good to me."

Vinnie and his mother agreed they would all meet at 7:30 and then Vinnie headed back inside his apartment.

Mercedes motioned to her mother, and the two women tiptoed to Shelby's front door. Carlita stuck the master key in the lock and unlocked the door. "Are we sure we want to do this?"

"Do we have a choice?"

"No. As much as I'm against invading a person's private space, we have to get to the bottom of what is going on." Carlita eased Shelby's door open.

The interior was dark, with only a small amount of light beaming through the slits in the living room blinds.

Mercedes reached for the light switch.

"Wait."

"What?" Mercedes lowered her hand. "We can't snoop if we can't see.

"True. Go ahead and turn the lights on."

Mercedes flipped the switch and bright light illuminated the tidy space.

Carlita took a step back to ease the door closed when she heard a sharp voice ring out from the hall.

"Hey!"

Chapter 16

Startled, Carlita spun around, coming face-to-face with Elvira. "What are you doing in here?"

"I forgot to ask you when you wanted to plan a visit to the Black Stallion. Your back door was locked, but it wasn't latched. You might wanna get that fixed. I pushed it open and walked right in."

"Great," Carlita grumbled. "Remind me to have Bob Lowman take a look at it, Mercedes."

Elvira craned her neck, peering over Carlita's shoulder. "You find anything yet?"

"We just got in here."

Elvira slipped past Carlita and entered Shelby's apartment. "This is a nice apartment. It looks bigger than my old apartment."

"All four of the apartments are identical with the exact same square footage."

"Huh." Elvira nodded. "I know you haven't asked for my opinion, but if I was going to search the place, I would start in the desk area, filing cabinets, something like that." She pointed to a small desk, located between the living room and the kitchen area.

"I'll do it." Mercedes hurried to the desk. On top was a vertical divider with several bills sticking out. Next to the desk was a file box. She lifted the lid. "There's nothing out of the ordinary in here, utility bills, bank statements, that kind of thing."

"Junk drawers can be goldmines." Elvira approached the kitchen cabinets. "I'll take a quick peek inside here for you." She pulled one of the drawers open. "Silverware."

"Oh brother." Carlita shook her head.

It was too late. Elvira was in her element as she began digging through the kitchen drawers.

Carlita was certain it would take longer to convince her former tenant to leave than it would to quickly search the place and get out.

"Don't destroy anything," Carlita warned.

Mercedes continued searching the desk area while Carlita headed to the small hall and the bedrooms in the back. There was a good chance they wouldn't find anything since Mercedes and Carlita had helped Shelby clean up earlier and hadn't noticed anything out of the ordinary.

Carlita did a quick visual search of Violet's pink and pastel princess bedroom before she moved on to the bathroom. She did a quick search of the medicine cabinet and the cabinet under the sink before heading to Shelby's bedroom.

The door was ajar, so Carlita nudged it open with the tip of her shoe and stepped inside. The bedroom light was already on and she hesitated for a fraction of a second as an internal war waged. She was uncomfortable invading what was not only her tenant's space, but also the private space of her son's girlfriend.

She took a tentative step to the right and the bedroom dresser. On top of the dresser was a glass bowl. Inside the bowl were hairpins, a bracelet, a pair of earrings and one silver key.

Carlita moved past the dresser to a folding chair propped against the wall. In front of the chair was a wicker laundry basket. She lifted the lid and peered into the empty basket before walking to the far side of the bed and the bedside table.

On top were a rainbow-colored stacked glass table lamp and a cork coaster. A quilted blue and yellow bedspread covered the bed and several small throw pillows were scattered along the headboard.

She retraced her steps, to the other side of the bed and the second bedside table where she found a matching table lamp and coaster. The room was clean...almost too clean, but then

Carlita reminded herself they had straightened the apartment right before they dropped Shelby off at her uncle's house.

She paused briefly, deciding whether to open the dresser drawers and take a quick look inside when she heard an excited yelp coming from the other room.

"Jackpot!"

Carlita hurried into the living room. "You found something?"

"Mercedes did. Check it out."

She joined her daughter and Elvira, who were standing at the bar staring at a piece of paper. "What is it?"

"Shelby's cell phone bill."

"Her cell phone bill is a clue?"

"Not the bill itself," Elvira explained. "It's the call log." She ran her finger down the list of numbers. "Do you recognize any of these numbers?"

Carlita squinted her eyes. "I don't have my reading glasses. I can't make heads or tails of the numbers."

"I can." Mercedes lifted the cell phone bill. "This is Tony's number, this is the pawnshop phone. I see your number Ma. There are a few I don't recognize."

"I'm sure one of them is the post office."

"There are several incoming calls that aren't local, and they're all within the last thirty days."

"It could be nothing," Carlita said.

"Or it could be something," Elvira said. "Think about it. You said yourself Shelby's ex didn't live in the area. How did he contact her?"

"I have no idea."

Elvira began to pace. "Here's my theory. Robert was somehow able to track Shelby here. He may have even gotten her cell phone number and called her."

"Shelby did say she met Robert. She never said anything about him showing up on her doorstep."

"Which means his first contact could have been via cell phone, unless she has a home phone."

"She doesn't," Mercedes said. "How are we going to figure out if any of these numbers is a clue?"

Elvira snorted. "It's a good thing I'm here to help. I need a cell phone."

Mercedes tugged her cell phone from her back pocket. "I have mine."

"Perfect. Take a picture of the phone log. When you get home, start calling the unidentified numbers."

"And tell them what? I'm Shelby's landlord; I broke into her apartment, snooped through her personal belongings and started calling everyone who contacted her over the last thirty days?"

"Of course not," Elvira snapped. "You make up some excuse. In fact, I have one I've been dying to try for a while now. May I?"

Mercedes reluctantly handed her cell phone to Elvira.

Elvira switched the phone on. "Where's the camera-thingy?"

"Here." Mercedes scrolled through the icons and tapped the screen.

"Perfect." Elvira shifted the phone away from the sheet of paper and pressed the button. "There are more numbers on the other side."

She flipped the sheet over and snapped a second picture. "This should be fairly easy, although I must say I'm surprised she has a paper copy of her cell phone records. Not many people request those anymore unless, of course, she's able to turn them in to her employer for reimbursement if she uses her cell phone for business purposes."

Mercedes tapped her mother's arm. "I told you we need to have a registered business name so it can start paying for some of our expenses. Between the pawnshop, the rental business and the restaurant, we need to make sure we're taking advantage of all of our legitimate write-offs."

"We'll look into it," Carlita promised. "Just as soon as we get this mess straightened out."

"That should be enough." Elvira handed Mercedes her cell phone. "Do you have time to call the people on the list tonight?"

Carlita glanced at her watch. "We're heading out shortly for a family dinner at some tapas restaurant downtown."

Elvira looked disappointed. "Crud. I was hoping we could test out my phone inquiry ruse. Are you busy tomorrow?"

"Mercedes is taking Brittney shoe shopping and I have another matter to take care of. We could do it first thing in the morning."

"Perfect. I have a new client meeting me at eleven. How does nine-thirty tomorrow morning sound?"

"Okay, I guess."

"Great. Come over to my place around nine-thirty tomorrow morning. We can run down this list faster than you can say Bibbidi-Bobbidi-Boo."

The trio exited the apartment after Carlita made sure all of the lights were off. She locked the door and pulled it shut, giving it a sharp tug to make sure it was closed.

"See you in the morning." Elvira tromped down the stairs, whistling a catchy tune. She gave them a jaunty wave before breezing out the back door.

Mercedes shook her head. "How does she do that?"

"Do what?"

"Take over. You told her we could handle the search. Next thing you know, not only is she helping us search, she's taken control of the investigation."

"That's Elvira. I would like to say we could've managed fine on our own, but I'm not sure I would've thought to go through Shelby's cell phone log to search for clues."

"Me either," Mercedes said. "We better hurry up and get ready or we're gonna be late."

Mother and daughter had just enough time to stop at their apartment to freshen up before meeting Tony, Vinnie, and Brittney downstairs.

Tony looked glum and Carlita was certain Shelby's situation was weighing heavy on her son's mind. "Any luck with the laptop?"

"No. I'm still working on it." Despite Tony's somber mood, he joined in the conversation as they meandered through the squares, making their way to the City Market.

"This is it." Vinnie stopped in front of one of the restaurants. "Brittney took a look at the online menu before we left the apartment."

Brittney studied the menu board on the wall near the entrance. "I have a few things I would like to try, if you don't mind."

"Of course not," Carlita said kindly. "It was very thoughtful of you to take a look at the menu ahead of time."

Brittney beamed at the compliment and a wave of guilt washed over Carlita. She hadn't been unkind to her new daughter-in-law, but then she hadn't been exactly warm and welcoming, either.

Of course, she placed some of the blame squarely on her eldest son's shoulders for springing the shocking surprise of his marriage to the mafia boss' daughter, for which she still planned to have a private chat with him.

Mercedes and Brittney's shopping trip would be the perfect opportunity to spend a few moments alone with her son.

Although the restaurant was busy, they were quickly seated at a table. Brittney was knowledgeable about the tapas menu, and Carlita complimented her several times on her selection of shared dishes. There was only one she didn't care for, and it was merely a personal preference since she wasn't much of a mussel lover, although the others seemed to enjoy it.

While they ate, they discussed the pawnshop, the apartment rentals and the restaurant renovations.

"You've done a great job, Ma. Brittney and I both agree the apartment is very nice and if we were in the market for an apartment, we would jump at the chance to rent yours."

"Thanks, son. We've worked hard to make sure our tenants are happy and it's a safe place to live." Shelby's break-in flitted through

Carlita's mind and she wondered if her tenant hadn't staged the break-in.

She quickly pushed the thought aside, determined to enjoy the evening with her family. While they ate, Vinnie filled them in on upcoming changes for the casino, his new job as the operations manager and Castellini's plans for casino expansion.

Carlita reached for her glass of water. "Castellini plans to purchase more casinos?"

"He would like to expand into the Georgia market. Vito has some connections he's working on, to have the issue placed on an upcoming ballot."

"Does Vito think he has a shot at getting a vote on the ballot?" Carlita asked.

"Yes, he does." Vinnie quickly changed the subject. "Mercedes is going to take you shoe shopping tomorrow," he told his wife.

"I can hardly wait." Brittney chattered on about the purchases she'd made that day, and then went into a long spiel touting the features of her favorite brand of designer shoes.

Carlita only half-listened as she thought about Vinnie's words and then she had another thought. "Son, you're not shopping with the girls tomorrow?"

"No, I have a small business matter to attend to," Vinnie said. "How about you? You going shopping with the girls?"

"No." Carlita stared at her eldest son thoughtfully. "I have a small matter to attend to in the morning, as well."

Chapter 17

"I have no idea how this woman talks us into doing what she wants us to do," Mercedes grumbled.

"Elvira does have a way about her." Carlita hurried to keep up with her daughter as they made their way down the sidewalk. "I have to admit I'm curious as to how she's going to trace Shelby's cell phone calls."

"Me too." They reached the front of Elvira's building and the EC Investigative Services entrance. "I give it a 50/50 chance of being illegal."

"Or sketchy at best."

"Yep." Carlita opened the door and they stepped inside the building where they found Elvira seated behind a desk, her head lowered as she concentrated on a file in front of her. She glanced up at the bell chime.

"Ah. Right on time." She flipped the folder shut and pushed it to the side. "Have a seat."

Mercedes slid into an empty chair facing Elvira and Carlita sat in the one next to her daughter.

Elvira swiveled in the chair and hollered, "Hey, Dernice! You ready?"

"Coming."

"Dernice is joining us?" Mercedes asked.

"Yeah. We're cross training. I show her some of the tricks for investigating; she fills me in on her security tips."

Dernice moseyed into the area. "Hello, ladies. Elvira tells me you've been busy spying on one of your tenants."

"We have not been spying," Carlita said.

"So you say. Not that it's any of my business." Dernice rolled an office chair across the room and plopped down. "Elvira said you have an ironclad rental agreement and your tenant would never win if she took you to court for trespassing."

"We were not trespassing," Mercedes insisted. "Elvira, you have a big mouth."

"Eh. I've been called worse." Elvira rubbed her hands together. "Let's get down to business. I don't have all day."

"Neither do we." Mercedes handed Elvira two folded sheets of paper. "I emailed the phone records to myself and then printed them off so they would be easier to read."

"Thanks." Elvira took the papers from her. "What are your cell phone numbers so I can cross them off the list?" She waved her hand. "Never mind. I have your cell phone numbers right here."

She pulled out her keyboard tray.

Carlita leaned forward. "You keep a printed list of cell phone numbers?"

"Yeah. I keep this handy when I don't want to fiddle with my cell phone." Elvira set the first sheet of paper next to her phone list.

She quickly cross-referenced the sheet, drawing red lines through some of the numbers. She repeated the steps with the second sheet. "That narrows down the list. Let's call the first number."

"I'll put it on speaker phone." Elvira lifted the desk phone receiver and punched the keys.

The line rang. "Savannah Post Office."

"Wrong number." Elvira disconnected the line. "That takes off a bunch more numbers." She redlined more of the sheet. "Let's try this one."

Elvira punched in another set of numbers.

"Savannah Preschool Center, Mary speaking."

"Sorry, wrong number." Elvira didn't wait for a reply and disconnected the line. "Two down, only a couple more to go." The others sat silently as Elvira tried the third number, this time a pizza place. She hung up on the man, who began rattling off the daily specials.

"We're running out of numbers." She dialed the next number. It rang several times before a man answered. "Hello?"

"Yes, uh." Elvira briefly hesitated. "This is Tina from radio station WIBS in the greater Atlanta area. Who am I speaking with?"

There was silence on the other end, and Carlita wondered if the person had hung up.

Undeterred, Elvira plunged into her spiel. "I'm calling to inform you that you've been randomly selected to receive a dozen free long-stemmed red roses, delivered to the location of your choice."

"Seriously?" the man asked.

"Absolutely. It's a pre-Valentine's Day promotional giveaway, offered by Flowers4u, a national floral company, who is promoting its new location in the Savannah area."

"Huh." The man wasn't convinced. "What's the catch?"

"No catch," Elvira said. "All I need from you is a name and address of where you would like to have the flowers sent. They can be sent to anywhere in the United States, and delivery will take place within the next 24-hours."

"Sure...uh. Send them to Kelsie Scott." The man rattled off an address in Richmond Hill, Georgia, and Elvira repeated it back. "Okay. I've got the information...and whose name should we put on the card?"

"You want my name?"

"Yes, unless you want the flowers sent anonymously, but then you can't take credit for such a generous gesture. Personally, I think you would want this special lady to know who sent the flowers."

"Yes. Of course. My name is Quinton Towns."

"Okay, Quinton. I have the information and as I said, the flowers will be sent out in the next 24-hours. Have a great day."

"Thank you."

Elvira disconnected the line. "Does Quinton Towns ring a bell?"

"No, but that's Shelby's last name. So someone who has the same last name recently called her cell phone."

"Let's wrap up this operation before we pore over what we've got." Elvira dialed the last few numbers on Shelby's cell phone list. One was a local drugstore, another rang but no one answered and the last had been disconnected.

"So our best lead is Quinton Towns." Elvira studied the cell phone log. "This log shows three incoming calls from Mr. Towns' number. All calls take place within a three day timeframe."

Carlita clasped her hands. "I'm even more confused than before. Robert is dead. If what you're saying is true, Shelby has been talking to her ex's relative."

"Let's take a lookee see at a coupla social media sites to see if we can get a visual on Quinton Towns. It's not a common name, so we should be able to easily find him, if he's on social media." Elvira slid her cell phone off to the side and began tapping on her computer keyboard.

"Nothing on this site." She reached for her mouse. "We got a Quinton Towns who lives in Richmond Hill." She clicked on the profile and double clicked on the picture. "It looks like we might have our stalker. Check it out."

She turned the laptop so Dernice, Mercedes and Carlita could see the screen. "I'll bet money this is the same guy who was lurking around the other day, the one I followed to the Black Stallion Club."

"Quinton Towns," Carlita murmured. "Who also called Shelby's cell phone and was lurking around when her apartment was broken into."

"He was probably looking for the backpack," Mercedes blurted out.

"Backpack?" Elvira perked up. "What backpack?"

"It's nothing," Carlita murmured.

"It's something to look into." Mercedes hopped out of her chair, anxious to avoid Elvira's impending interrogation. "It's getting late and I'm sure Brittney is ready to head out on our shoe shopping excursion."

"Barbie?" Dernice asked. "I figured your son and his gal were already gone. I haven't seen them around."

"They're leaving soon." Carlita slid out of her chair. "That was very clever, Elvira, and a sneaky way to get someone to reveal their name. How did you think of that?"

"I heard it on a radio program a coupla years ago. The program's host had female listeners who thought their boyfriends or husbands were cheating on them call in." According to Elvira, the women would give the talk show host the boyfriend or husband's name and contact information.

The talk show host would then call them on the phone, all the while airing the calls live while the women were listening in. They somehow convinced the men they were from a flower shop and were randomly calling individuals to send complimentary bouquets of flowers to the recipient of their choice.

"Half the men sent the flowers to the woman secretly listening on the other end, but the other half?" Elvira blew air through thinned lips. "Those cheating dogs were outed right there on the radio and those women were ticked. I would hate to have been some of them when the women got their hands on the cheaters."

"Well, now you know it works." Carlita reached for the phone records.

"It's one of my methods to track down valuable information. I have many more up my sleeve. So what's the next step? Are you going to confront Shelby and ask her who Quinton Towns is?"

"It's on my to-do list, Elvira, but not this morning. I have something else to take care of first."

Elvira followed them to the door. "What about our fact-finding trip to the Black Stallion? We could run by there this evening."

"Yes, I guess it couldn't hurt," Carlita said.

"Perfect." Elvira rubbed her hands together. "Let's rendezvous at eighteen hundred hours in the alley."

"Which is?"

"Six o'clock."

"Sure." Carlita thanked her again, for helping them sift through Shelby's phone records and then they stepped onto the sidewalk.

Mercedes waited until the door was closed. "What do you think?"

"The waters are getting murkier by the minute. I tossed and turned all night thinking about it. After this morning's phone calls, Shelby is obviously hiding something and I agree with Elvira. I think the man lurking about was Quinton Towns."

"You keep saying you have something to take care of." Carlita began walking and Mercedes fell into step. "Let me guess...you're going to follow Vinnie to see what kind of business he has to take care of."

"That's one plan. I also tossed around the idea of asking Vinnie for his help. Vinnie already has knowledge of the Black Stallion if what Elvira claims is true and she saw him there. I don't know what he's planning for today, but maybe I can talk to him privately and ask him what's going down at the Black Stallion."

"He might not be willing to help you Ma," Mercedes pointed out. "The family code of honor and all that jazz. It would be considered a conflict of interest."

"True. The last thing I want to do is put one of my sons on the wrong side of the family."

"Maybe a better bet is to follow Vinnie, and then later meet with Shelby and ask her about Quinton."

"I see your point and you're right. Still, I need to find out for myself what Vinnie is up to." Carlita sighed heavily. It had been a long few days and it felt like her world was crumbling around her. Tony and Shelby, Vinnie's surprise marriage and Vinnie's new job, working for the head of the mafia.

"I say we don't jump to conclusions," Mercedes suggested. "We still need to figure out how the cash we found in the backpack, the Harner Street property and the Black Stallion Club are related."

The women stopped by the pawnshop to chat with Tony, where they found Vinnie and Brittney.

Brittney's eyes lit when she spied Mercedes. "I'm ready to go."

"Me too."

Carlita handed Mercedes the car keys. "You don't need the car for your...errand?"

"Uh, I hadn't thought of that." Carlita had no idea where Vinnie was headed. Her eldest son wasn't much of a walker, and she was almost certain wherever he was going, he would drive.

"You can take my Segway. The helmet is hanging on the handlebars."

"I'm not sure about that, Mercedes. You know I'm still not comfortable tooling around on it."

Mercedes had taught her mother how to navigate around their neighborhood on the Segway, but that was the extent of her comfort level.

"You might not have a choice."

Mercedes was right. If Vinnie drove off in his car and Mercedes took their car, Carlita's only means of transportation would be Tony's car, a vehicle Vinnie would easily recognize. The Segway would give Carlita the ability to stay under the radar. If, however, Vinnie headed out of town and onto the highway, she would be out of luck.

Vinnie would never suspect his mother trailing after him on the two-wheeler. "You're right Mercedes. I might have to borrow your Segway."

Mercedes squeezed her mother's arm. "You can do it. Just keep an eye out for the uneven bricks. They'll throw you for a loop if you're not careful. Oh, and watch out for the touristas. They never pay attention to where they're going and have a bad habit of walking right into your path."

"Great. Maybe I should forget about the whole thing."

Brittney listened quietly to the exchange. "I'm not sure I would want to get on one of those Segways. They look tippy. You can always go shoe shopping with us."

"I appreciate your offer, Brittney. Maybe next time."

Vinnie made his way over. "You two ladies heading out?"

"We are." Mercedes held up the car keys and gave them a quick shake. "We should only be a couple of hours. Do you want us to bring some food back?"

"Sure. Whatever Brittney wants," Vinnie leaned forward and gave his wife a smooch.

"You're so sweet," Brittney gushed.

"Sickeningly sweet," Mercedes muttered.

"Mercedes," Carlita chided.

"I'm kidding. Let's go." Mercedes and Brittney exited through the back of the store and Tony wandered over. "Has Shelby stopped by yet?"

"I haven't seen her. I'm not sure how long she plans to stay at her aunt and uncle's place."

"She called earlier to say she was going to run by the apartment and pick up a few more things, so I guess she won't be home tonight either." Tony massaged the back of his neck. "I tried to bring up the subject of her ex, to see if she heard anything else from the investigators. She shut me down."

"She has a lot on her mind, son. Give her time," Carlita said softly.

"Speaking of time, I gotta get goin'." Vinnie glanced at his watch. "I'm gonna be late for my appointment."

Vinnie strolled out of the store and Carlita started to follow behind.

Tony reached out to stop her. "Something is up with Vinnie. He keeps talking about this business deal. When I ask him what kind, he clams up, claiming it's nothing. Do you know what he's up to?"

"No, I don't, but just between the two of us I think it's time for me to find out."

Chapter 18

By the time Carlita reached the back hall, Vinnie was long gone. She stepped into the alley and spied his car still parked in the parking lot.

She cast a glance toward the top of the stairs and then at Mercedes' Segway, sitting off to the side, next to Tony's apartment.

Carlita shoved her keys in her pocket and pulled Mercedes' helmet off the handle before steering the Segway into the alley. Thankfully, there was still no sign of Vinnie.

After slipping the helmet on, she gingerly climbed onto the contraption. "Forward to go forward, straight up to stop and there is no brake," she reminded herself.

Carlita eased the handlebars forward and the Segway rolled along the rutted alley. She coasted to the end and shifted the handle to the right, making a wide U-turn.

After successfully making two trips up and down the alley, she hopped off and then steered the Segway into a narrow doorway, not far from the end of the alley.

She peeked around the corner, which gave her an unobstructed view of the alley door. Carlita remained hidden for what seemed like forever, waiting for Vinnie to appear.

Finally, Carlita's oldest son emerged from the building. He pulled the door shut and then strode to the parking lot at the other end.

Carlita tiptoed forward, far enough to keep an eye on him. The car's engine revved and loose gravel crunched under the tires as he backed out of the parking spot.

She watched as his dark sedan coasted to the corner and stopped for a minute, before slowly pulling onto the street.

"Here goes nothing." Carlita sprang into action and steered the Segway to the end of the alley where she climbed on the footrests and gripped the handlebars. She could see Vinnie's car up ahead, idling at the stop sign. He slowly pulled away and when he did, Carlita eased the handlebars forward.

Vinnie turned left at the next corner before making a quick right onto another side street.

Carlita went as fast as she dared, but hung back as far as she could, praying her son wouldn't notice her.

He drove back and forth, up and down the side streets, and she began to wonder if Vinnie was lost. Finally, he turned onto a street that ran parallel to River Street, a main thoroughfare that ran along the Savannah River.

Vinnie made one more turn and then eased his car into an empty parking spot.

Carlita steered the Segway between two buildings and hopped off. She ran to the corner and caught a glimpse of her son as he stepped into a building and disappeared from sight.

"What is he doing?" She climbed back on the Segway and sped along the street toward her son's car. She slowed when she got close, hoping to catch a glimpse of the building he'd gone into.

She did a double take when she read the sign on the front of the building: *Savannah Office of Business Development.*

***

Mercedes nodded absentmindedly as her sister-in-law chattered on about the penthouse apartment renovations. "I told Vin we should plant an herb garden on the terrace. There's plenty of room. I've been thinking that you know, we want to have children soon and we need to watch what we eat."

"That sounds reasonable," Mercedes said. "Ma grows some tomatoes and herbs out on our balcony. Maybe she can give you some pointers."

"That would be awesome. Once our renovations are finished, you and your mother will have to come for a visit. We'll have plenty of room for company. Our unit was a two bedroom, two bath. Daddy gave us the one next to it, so we knocked out a few walls and combined the two."

"It sounds lovely," Mercedes said politely.

Brittney jabbered on about moving to New Jersey. "Mom wasn't too keen on me moving to Jersey, but I think she's finally coming around."

Mercedes interrupted. "I guess I never thought to ask - do you have any siblings?"

"Yes. I have...had two brothers. Tommy is my older brother. He runs Daddy's other casino." Brittney's normally sunny expression vanished, replaced by a troubled look. "My other brother, Dean, died a couple of years ago." She glanced at her hands in her lap. "We don't talk about it."

"I'm sorry."

"Me too," Brittney said in a small voice.

Mercedes decided to steer the conversation to a safer subject. "What is your favorite thing about Savannah so far?"

"Oh, the architecture. I love Savannah's architecture and history. I would love to take one of those haunted ghost tours, but Vinnie refuses."

"Maybe next time you visit, we can go on one. We're here," Mercedes announced.

After parking the car, the women made a beeline for the first shoe shop Brittney spotted.

Mercedes was ready to go after the first half an hour, but the outlet mall was loaded with shoe stores and Brittney was like a kid in a candy store. They shopped from one end of the mall to the other and along the way; Brittney purchased several pairs of shoes.

Finally, Brittney had shopped at every single shoe store and seemed satisfied with her purchases.

They returned to the car and Mercedes loaded the bags into the trunk.

"Thank you for taking me shopping. I don't think you had as much fun shopping as I did."

"It was okay," Mercedes said. "I'm not much of a shopper." She climbed into the driver's seat.

Brittney slid into the passenger seat and reached for her seatbelt. "I learned one thing today. If Daddy expands his casino business and asks Vinnie to come down here to run it, I'll have plenty of places to buy my shoes."

"Yes, you will." On the way back to the apartment, Mercedes swung by one of the local fast food restaurants where she picked up several burgers, orders of fries and sodas.

Vinnie's car was parked in the lot and the first thing Mercedes did when she stepped into the hall was check to see if her Segway was there. Her shoulders sagged with relief when she found it parked in the same spot.

Mercedes helped Brittney carry her purchases to the apartment and then carried the bags of fast food to the apartment where she found her mother seated at her desk.

"Hey, Ma. Did you take the Segway out?"

Carlita shifted in the chair. "I did and either I'm getting better at maneuvering on the contraption or I got lucky."

"Well?" Mercedes reached into the bag and pulled out a French fry. "Where did Vinnie go?"

"To the Savannah Office of Business Development. The name on the door was Emmett Pridgen. He's some kind of head of the downtown development committee."

"Brittney told me her father hopes to open a business here in Savannah."

The doorbell rang, interrupting their conversation and Mercedes headed for the door. "That's probably Brittney. I forgot to give her their food." She swung the door open to find Shelby standing on the other side.

"Hi, Shelby."

"Hi, Mercedes."

Carlita scooted out of her chair and joined her daughter at the door.

"I'm sorry to bother you. I stopped by my apartment to pick up a few more things. I'm almost certain someone was inside my apartment and I wondered if you noticed anything."

Carlita said the first thing that popped into her head. "Oh dear, Shelby. Was anything taken?"

"Not that I can tell."

Mercedes leaned her hip on the doorframe. "What makes you think someone was inside your apartment?"

"I left my bedroom light on and when I got there, the light was off."

"Maybe the bulb burned out," Mercedes suggested.

"The switch was off. The light works."

Carlita remembered turning off all of the lights inside Shelby's apartment after Elvira, Mercedes and she had finished searching it the previous night.

She didn't want to lie to Shelby, so Carlita decided her best bet was to change the subject. "How is it going at your uncle's place? Have you heard back from the post office on when you can return to work?"

"No." Shelby's face fell. "I left a message for my supervisor this morning, but haven't heard a peep. I got a call from the investigators this morning. They want me to come in to answer more questions."

"At least they're not showing up on your doorstep with an arrest warrant," Mercedes said.

"Do you have a minute, Shelby?" Carlita opened the door wider and smiled. "There's something I would like to talk to you about."

Shelby noted the solemn expression on Carlita's face and her chin started to quiver. "You're not going to evict me and Violet, are you?"

"I hope not," Carlita said. "Please. Come in."

Shelby clutched her purse and took a tentative step inside the apartment.

Carlita led the young woman to the dining room table and pulled out a chair. She decided a direct approach was best. "Who is Quinton Towns?"

"How do you know about Quinton?"

"Elvira took a picture of a man who was lurking around the apartment building the same day your apartment was ransacked. She did a little research and found out the man's name is Quinton Towns."

"Quinton is Robert's brother. He called my cell phone and asked to meet with me. I told the authorities he was harassing me, but I don't think they took me seriously."

"Do you think Quinton might be involved in Robert's death?"

"It's possible. He said something about some missing money. I don't trust Quinton." Shelby clasped her hands. "Now that I think about it, he also mentioned someone by the name of Pat, just like Robert."

"I need to get going." Shelby glanced at her watch. "I borrowed my uncle's truck and he's probably starting to worry."

Carlita walked Shelby to the door and waited until she was gone before turning to her daughter. "We now have one more mystery person...Pat."

Chapter 19

Mercedes headed to her room while Carlita grabbed Brittney and Vinnie's fast food and walked over to their apartment.

The hall was quiet, and Carlita shifted the bags of food to her other hand before rapping lightly on the apartment door. She heard movement from within. The door opened and Vinnie emerged.

"This is yours." Carlita handed him the bags of food. "Mercedes said she and Brittney had fun shopping."

"You should see the load of loot Brittney came home with."

"I hope you can afford her shopping habit," Carlita chuckled.

"We're fine. If Brittney's happy, then I'm happy."

"Carlita studied Vinnie's expression. He did seem happy and even though she was disappointed to discover he was moving to New Jersey instead of Savannah, his happiness was what was important. The only problem she had with the situation was her son was now related to a mafia boss.

If nothing else, Atlantic City would put a little distance between the couple and the "family," at least that's what Carlita hoped would be the case. "Were you able to take care of your errand earlier today?"

"Yeah. I did my part." Vinnie shrugged. "Now it's up to Vito to handle the rest. My work here is done and now it's time for Brittney and me to head north."

"You still plan on leaving in the morning?"

"Yeah. We're heading out early. It's about a twelve-hour drive from here, so I want to be on the road by six tomorrow morning."

"That is early."

"We'll load the car tonight, but I figured we could get together for dinner if you want."

"Of course. How about if I whip up one of your favorite Italian dinners?"

"Spaghetti and meatballs," Vinnie guessed.

"Yes. I have some errands to take care of at six. In the meantime, I'll whip up some spaghetti and meatballs and have them ready later this evening."

"That sounds good, Ma."

Brittney emerged from the apartment. "I thought I heard voices. How do you like my new shoes?" She squeezed past her husband and wobbled into the hall. "These are my new favorite pair. They're Christian Louboutin."

She tilted her foot and modeled the gray-green mini spike stiletto heels.

"Those are nice," Carlita said. "You wouldn't catch me wearing them. I would break my neck."

"They look expensive. How much for this pair Brit?" Vinnie waved his hand, not giving his wife a chance to answer. "Never mind. I'm sure I don't want to know."

Brittney blew Vinnie a kiss and tottered back inside the apartment.

"I'll let you go, son. What do you say we have dinner around seven-thirty at my place? It will give Tony a few minutes to clean up after he closes the store."

"Sounds good, Ma."

With dinner plans in place, Carlita returned to the apartment. Before she stepped inside, she glanced at Shelby's apartment door. She was on the fence about confessing to the young woman that she, along with Mercedes and Elvira, had snooped.

Surely, Shelby was curious to know how Carlita and Mercedes knew about Quinton. She quickly decided it was best to let it go for now.

Carlita pulled the ground beef from the fridge to start making the meatballs. After mixing the ingredients and forming the balls, she stacked them inside a bowl, covered it with plastic and placed it in the fridge.

Mercedes hurried into the kitchen. "I did a little digging around on Emmett Pridgen, the business development guy Vinnie paid a visit to earlier. The guy is shadier than a palm tree."

"Really?" Carlita hung her apron on the hook near the pantry. "Shady as in how?"

"Maybe not shady, but definitely suspicious. He's only been a member of the city council for about a year. In that short amount of time, he's spearheaded several special interest projects including the downtown warehouse project, which tentatively includes a casino gambling venue."

"Gambling isn't legal in Georgia," Carlita said.

"Ah, and that is where you're wrong. There's a gambling boat in South Georgia. I'm not sure of the exact location. The gambling boat travels out far enough to hit international waters and then the passengers are allowed to gamble."

"So this Emmett Pridgen is trying to open a gambling boat in Savannah. It doesn't make him a criminal."

"Pridgen was investigated for allegedly accepting kickbacks in Atlanta for some business dealings. The case was headed to trial until the lead investigator, a man by the name of Mason, mysteriously vanished and the case was dropped."

"Pridgen killed him?" Carlita asked.

"That's my theory, but it's hard to prosecute when there's no body."

"The investigator, Mason, never surfaced?"

"Nope." Mercedes shook her head. "Dead or alive."

"So you think this city official, Pridgen, may be responsible for Robert Towns' death?" Carlita asked.

"It makes sense. I'm not ruling out anyone, including Quinton Towns."

"Don't forget Vito Castellini and his 'associates.' I don't understand how Robert was involved and there's still the mystery of the backpack and cash. I sure wish we could figure out who owns the Harner Street property."

"Well, that's the other thing I found out. We know it's owned by East Coast Ventures. Annie told us that. What we need now are the partners' names. If we can figure out who owns the property, I think we'll have another piece of the puzzle."

"How do we do that?" Carlita asked.

"Skip trace." Mercedes explained skip tracing was an online service used to track down fugitives or people wanted by the law. "You can also use it to find out *who* owns specific property."

"We could ask Elvira."

"I already thought about that. If Elvira operated a skip tracer service, she would've offered it to us by now, for a fee, of course." Mercedes tapped her chin. "I was thinking we could ask Annie. She might know someone who has a skip tracing service, especially since she works in the real estate business."

"I saw Annie's car in front of her office earlier. Why don't we run over there to see if she can help?"

"Let's do it." Mercedes ran to her room to grab her cell phone and met her mother in the hall. "I feel good about this. I think we're about to crack this case wide open."

Carlita cast a glance at Shelby's apartment door. "Hopefully, it leads us to someone other than Shelby. C'mon Rambo."

"Right?" Mercedes bounded down the steps and Carlita and Rambo followed behind.

"Before we do that, let's see if Tony was able to crack the code on the laptop." Carlita stepped into the back of the pawnshop. The store was empty and she spotted her son sitting at the desk, staring at a computer screen.

"Is this the computer we found?" Carlita said in her son's ear.

Tony jumped. "You scared me half to death."

"Sorry, son. Were you able to unlock the laptop?"

"No. I tried a hundred different combinations. So far nothing is working."

"Annie is a whiz with technical stuff. We could ask her to try to unlock the computer."

"It's worth a shot," Tony said. "It's hard for me to focus on it in between helping customers."

A customer entered the store. "See?" Tony shut the laptop and handed it to his mother.

"Thanks for trying, son."

Rambo led them out of the pawnshop and onto the sidewalk out front.

A gentle breeze blew around the side of the building and Carlita gazed up at the clear blue skies. "What a beautiful day."

"Yes, it is," Mercedes agreed. "It would be a perfect day to solve a mystery."

Chapter 20

Carlita caught a glimpse of Cindy, Annie's assistant, sitting at her desk, but there was no sign of Annie.

Cindy waited for the women to step into the real estate office. "Hello, ladies...and Rambo."

Rambo trotted across the room to greet Cindy and she gave him a quick pat on the head before reaching into her desk drawer where she pulled out a small box of doggie treats and gave one to the pooch.

Rambo rewarded her with a hand lick before accepting the treat and plopping down on the floor to enjoy it.

"Annie is in the conference room, finishing up with a client. Is there something I can help you with?"

"Maybe," Carlita said. "I'll let Mercedes explain."

"We need to find someone who offers skip tracing services."

"To track down a property owner?"

"Exactly." Mercedes nodded.

"I think Annie might know someone. Did you check with Elvira? I would think with her investigative services company, she would have access to skip tracing."

"We haven't. We decided to ask Annie first."

"...and I'll touch base with you tomorrow." Annie and a woman emerged from the back and they walked to the front door. "I'm sure we'll be able to find you the perfect property."

The woman thanked Annie and exited the office.

"Two visits in one week." Annie crossed the room. "What's the occasion?"

"We need your help again," Carlita said. "We're looking for someone who offers skip tracing services."

"Oh." Annie lifted a brow.

"We're hoping a skip trace might help us track down the names of the owners of the Harner Street property." Carlita placed the password-locked laptop on the desk. "We were also hoping that you and your mad scientist creative-mind would be able to help us unlock this laptop."

"You don't have the password?"

Carlita and Mercedes exchanged a glance. "It...doesn't belong to us. We want to know what's on it."

"I see. Well, the less I know the better." Annie pulled the computer to her and lifted the lid. "This has a fairly simple locking system. The laptop appears to be a couple of years old." She tapped the screen. "It might take a minute."

"Take your time."

"And...okay, I've got it." Annie hummed under her breath as she searched the laptop.

"What did you do?" Mercedes leaned forward.

Annie grinned. "I can't give away *all* of my secrets. I learned a lot on the internet while building my robot, Tinker." She grew quiet. "Hmm... About the only thing on this computer is a booking site."

"Booking?" Carlita asked.

"It's an online website." Annie went on to explain the program operated a lot like financial software. "I heard about this a while back. It's actually pretty slick. The bookie directs his clients to a website, where bets are recorded, tracked and totaled. The bookie can then log on to see who owes — or is owed — money in the coming week."

"So it's legal online gambling?" Carlita asked.

"No way." Annie shook her head. "It's illegal as all get-out. Most of these companies are overseas, so they're hard to track. If the bookie keeps moving, it's almost impossible for the authorities to catch them."

"We suspect the laptop belonged to Robert, Shelby's ex, but we can't be certain," Carlita confessed.

"There's something else on here." Annie tapped the keys. "You won't need a skip trace service after all." She turned the laptop.

Carlita squinted her eyes. "What am I looking at?"

"It's a copy of the deed for 412 Harner Street, owned by East Coast Ventures. The second line lists the owner's name."

"Robert," Carlita whispered.

Mercedes peered over her mother's shoulder. "This ties the property to Robert, along with the money we found. What if Robert owed someone money and they took him out?"

"This still doesn't tie into the Black Stallion or explain why Quinton Towns has been snooping around our place," Carlita said.

"We know Quinton was Robert's brother. For some reason, Quinton didn't know about the Harner Street property, so he came after Shelby, thinking Robert had given her the cash we found in the backpack."

"You two have been busy," Annie said.

"I think we should go ahead with the skip tracing to verify the ownership of Harner Street," Mercedes said.

"This proves Robert owns the property." Carlita jabbed her finger at the laptop.

"No, it doesn't." Mercedes stubbornly shook her head.

After a brief stare down, Carlita relented. "Go ahead with the skip trace."

Annie moved the laptop off to the side and turned her attention to her computer. "I have a colleague at another real estate company who offers skip tracing as a side business. I used it a few months ago to track down a deadbeat tenant for a friend."

"How much does it cost?" Carlita asked.

"If it's a simple online search and the information is easily located, I think I paid about a hundred bucks."

"A hundred dollars," Carlita gasped. "I'm not sure I want the information that badly."

"Yes, we do." Mercedes frowned at her mother. "We do want the information."

Carlita muttered something unintelligible under her breath. "Okay, but we're not going to pay more than a hundred dollars."

"Let me make a quick phone call." Annie reached for her cell phone and Mercedes motioned to her mother. "We have to clear Shelby's name and Vinnie's for that matter. Think about it. You saw Vinnie enter a city office. Ten bucks says he was meeting with Emmett Pridgen to maybe grease his palms for Castellini and move the casino boat project along. What if Pridgen is a killer?"

"How does this involve Robert and Quinton Towns?" Carlita asked.

"My theory is Pridgen and the Towns brothers worked together to set up a scam, or maybe it wasn't even a scam, to find investors interested in investing in the casino boat venture. They targeted established casino owners, including those in Atlantic City and Vito Castellini. Robert purchased the property under an LLC so that he had some weight with city officials as a property owner, and then the trio started luring in the investors."

Carlita picked up. "Robert got greedy. If they were messing with the mafia, they were playing with fire and Robert got burned."

"I bet there's also some sort of connection to the Black Stallion Club. Which reminds me, we need to ask Annie if she can tell us who owns the club."

"Hey." Annie covered her cell phone. "It's gonna be seventy-five dollars for a quickie skip trace. Yes or no?"

"Ugh. Yes," Carlita said. "I'm going to write this off as a business expense. Can they send me a bill?"

"Can you run the trace and then send me the bill?" Annie paused. "Yeah. I can vouch for my client. Good. Okay. Call me back when you finish the trace." Annie thanked the person on the other end and then disconnected the call. "He said the search will only take about ten minutes, tops."

"We'll wait here if you don't mind," Carlita said. "We also wondered if you could tell us who owns the Black Stallion Club. We think there may be a link."

"Sure. I can check while we're waiting." Annie clicked the keys. "The Black Stallion has been around for as long as I can remember. It's kind of a rough joint. The place has had its share of black eyes, the occasional brawl, arrests and a few drug busts, but nothing serious enough to shut them down."

Annie's eyes grew wide. "Yeah, I got something."

Annie's cell phone chimed. "Hang on a sec. That's the skip tracer." She picked up the phone. "Annie Dowton speaking. Yes. Great. What did you find?" Annie reached for her pen. "Can you repeat that?"

She started scribbling furiously on her notepad and Mercedes lunged forward as she attempted to read what Annie was writing.

"I think this is exactly what we were looking for. Go ahead and email the invoice to me along with the other piece of information linked to the Harner Street property. Thank you. I'll be on the lookout for it."

"I can't stand this." Cindy hopped out of her chair and hustled to Annie's desk. She peeked over Annie's shoulder to read the words her boss had jotted down.

Annie held up the scratch pad to show them the list of names. "This is the owner of East Coast Ventures, and the owner of 412 Harner Street."

"We still have one more piece of pertinent information for you to look at before you start tossing out theories," Annie warned. "Let me print off what I found on the Black Stallion Club." The printer began to hum.

"I'll grab it." Cindy darted to the printer and pulled off the two sheets of paper. She handed them to Annie.

Annie took a quick glance at the papers. "The skip trace bill is on the bottom. Take a look at the top sheet."

Carlita took the sheets from Annie. The print was small and she didn't have her reading glasses, so she handed them to Mercedes. "What is this?"

Mercedes studied the sheet. "The Harner Street property is...was owned by Robert Towns."

"There's something else." Annie slid a second sheet of paper in front of them. "This is the name of the owner of the Black Stallion."

Carlita's breath caught in her throat. "Pat," she whispered.

"Pat Duce," Annie confirmed.

"I think this is confirmation that we need to pay a visit to the Black Stallion," Mercedes said.

Annie's eyes lit. "Can I tag along?"

"Of course. I have to warn you Elvira will be with us."

"That's fine." Annie waved a hand. "I can handle Elvira."

"I'm not sure anyone can handle Elvira."

Chapter 21

"I don't like the looks of this place." Carlita eyed the flashing neon sign above the entrance to the Black Stallion Club.

She turned to Annie. "You sure you don't want to change your mind?"

"No." Annie shook her head and swallowed hard. "This place isn't in the best part of town, but I'm good to go."

"This place is a dump," Elvira said. "Keep in mind we're not here to critique the charm and allure of the establishment." She turned to Mercedes. "You packing heat?"

"No. I tried, but Ma pointed out if the doorman searches us or our purses and finds a weapon, they will turn us away."

"I guess we'll have to take our chances and keep a low profile." Elvira squared her shoulders and marched to the front entrance.

Carlita followed Elvira, and Mercedes and Annie brought up the rear.

The doorman's arm shot out, almost clotheslining Elvira. "Hang on."

Elvira batted at his arm. "What seems to be the problem?"

"I need to check your ID."

Elvira reached into her front pocket and pulled out her driver's license. "Check my ID? I can tell you one thing, I'm over twenty-one."

"I'm sure you are." The man glanced at the driver's license and handed it back. "There's a five-dollar cover charge."

"You charge five bucks just to walk into this dump?" Elvira gasped.

Carlita shoved her hand into her purse and pulled out her wallet. "I've got the money." She handed the man a twenty-dollar bill. "There are four of us."

The man took the twenty. "The cover charge is for the jazz band Smooth Sully and the River Rats."

"They suck," Elvira snarled. "Cool Bones and the Jazz Boys are ten times better."

"No one is forcing you inside." The man glared at Elvira and she scowled back, grumbling under her breath as she stepped out of the way.

"Let it go Elvira," Carlita warned. "Remember, we're not here to cause a scene."

"Right." Elvira led them past the bar, circled around the front of the stage and then pointed to an empty table near the back. "Over there. I'll take the seat facing out."

She plunked down in the chair and motioned to the others. "You'll have to slide back so I have an unobstructed view of the patrons."

Carlita lifted a brow, but did as Elvira said and pushed her chair back to avoid blocking her line of vision.

Annie took the seat on the other side and Mercedes wiggled into the one next to her. "What's the plan?"

"Our first step is merely to sit back and observe, but a beer might help pass the time. Hey!" Elvira waved the server over. "I'd like to order a round of Bud Lights and my friend over there," pointing at Carlita, "is paying."

"Me?" Carlita gasped. "Oh no you don't. I'll take a Diet Coke instead."

"Me too," Annie nodded.

"Make it three," Mercedes said.

"Party poopers," Elvira scoffed. "Make that one bottle of Bud Light and don't give me one of those nasty tin cans."

"Coming right up." The server turned on her heel and disappeared into the crowd.

"You're drinking on the job?" Carlita wagged her finger at Elvira.

"It's not like the boss is going to fire me." Elvira chuckled at her own joke, but no one else joined in. "Oh, lighten up you guys."

The round of drinks arrived promptly, and Carlita unwrapped her straw and stuck it in the glass. "Show Annie the pictures you took earlier, so she has a general idea of the person we may be looking for."

Elvira set her beer down and reached in her pocket. She switched her cell phone on and then handed it to Annie, who was sitting next to her. "It's not a clear shot."

"This is the guy Elvira spotted lurking around outside our apartment right around the time Shelby's apartment was ransacked. She followed him here to the Black Stallion. We're certain it was Quinton Towns, Robert's brother."

Annie handed the phone back and glanced around. "Now I know why I've never been in here before."

The women sipped their drinks, all of them focusing their attention on the patrons inside the bar.

After an hour passed, the band began setting up. They started to play a familiar tune, one Carlita was sure she heard Cool Bones practice in his apartment. She had to agree Cool Bones and the Jazz Boys were much better than the River Rats.

When the group started their second song, she was certain Cool Bones was better, to the point that her head was starting to pound.

Carlita glanced at her watch. "How much longer before we call it a day? I have to be home by seven-thirty."

"Or else what? You turn into a pumpkin?" Elvira smirked. "We're just getting started." The server started to pass by the table. "I'll have another Bud." She waved her beer bottle at the woman. "That and an order of chicken wings and chips and salsa."

"I am kinda hungry," Annie said. "I love chicken wings."

"That's my girl," Elvira nodded approvingly. "We'll have one of each and don't skimp on the portions."

Carlita glanced at her almost empty glass of Diet Coke. "I might as well order another Diet Coke. I need to text Tony and Vinnie and warn them we might be a little late."

After the server left, Carlita turned to Elvira. "When the food is gone, we're going to head out with or without you."

"It's a deal." Elvira lifted her nearly empty bottle of beer and then quickly set it back down. "Ladies, I think we just hit pay dirt."

Chapter 22

"Over there." Elvira nodded her head toward the edge of the dance floor. "That's the guy I saw snooping around out behind your apartment. I would bet my life on it."

"Where?" Carlita squinted her eyes and scanned the crowded barroom floor.

"At eleven o'clock, to the left of the piano and in front of the dartboard."

The brown-haired man casually propped his elbow on the corner of the bar and surveyed the crowd. A heat crept up Carlita's neck as he paused, his attention focused on the women at the table.

She let out a sigh of relief when he continued his study of the crowd before turning his attention to the bartender, who set a drink in front of him.

The server returned a short time later carrying a large tray. She slid the edge of the tray on the table, and transferred the drinks, the basket of wings and the chips and salsa to the table. "Can I get you anything else?"

"Nope. I think that'll do 'er." Elvira reached for a small plate, scooped three wings onto it and passed the plate of food to Annie. "Ten bucks says he's not here to listen to the band, not that I would, either. They suck."

"Elvira," Carlita chided. "How would you like someone to say that about you?"

Elvira dipped her wing in the blue cheese dressing and shrugged. "They do. You should read the online reviews for EC Security Services." She bit into the wing, the hot sauce dripping down her chin.

"The reviews are mostly employee-related, so I put Dernice in charge of customer service training for our crew. They're a hardworking bunch, although a little rough around the edges. With the right training, they'll be polished and operating like a well-oiled machine."

Mercedes snorted. "What kind of bad reviews?"

"For the record, you can't believe everything you read. I'm sure some of the reviews are from my competitor, 'Savannah Security Services.'"

Elvira took another bite of her drumette. "One fakeroo reviewer claimed they caught my employee sleeping on the job. Another said an employee left their post to grab a bite to eat." She shook her head. "Of course they stepped out to grab some grub. I'm not running a prison camp."

Elvira polished off her first chicken wing and reached for a tortilla chip. "Back to our investigation. I thought about stationing someone near the exit, so that if our guy takes off we can follow him to find out where he goes."

"I hadn't thought of that," Carlita said. "Maybe we should've picked a table by the door instead."

"Bad idea," Elvira said. "There's a rear exit. I noticed it when we came in. From this vantage point, I can see the front exit and the rear exit. We'll have to hustle once we see him flying the coop, so you better chow down. I don't want to leave good food behind."

The server stopped at the table next door and Elvira waited until she finished taking their order. "Hey, blondie!" she hollered.

The server approached the table. "My name is Holly. What do you need?"

"She needs the check for the food and drinks." Elvira pointed to Carlita.

"Sure." Holly opened her notepad, ripped off a ticket and set it on the table. "I can take it up whenever you're ready."

Carlita picked up the bill and studied the charges. "Thirteen dollars for thirteen chicken wings? Good grief." She fumbled in her purse, pulled out her wallet and placed her debit card on top of the bill.

"That's only a buck a wing, not a bad price for a downtown joint." Elvira reached for another wing. "I hate to admit it, but they're not half bad." She dipped her wing in the dressing again. The wing was halfway to her mouth, and she paused mid-air. "Looks like our guy has company."

The women turned their attention to the bar and watched as another man approached the bar and squeezed in next to their target. He rapped his knuckles on the bar top and the bartender wandered over.

The new arrival nodded and shook hands with the bartender before the man reached under the bar and set a cold one on top.

"Great," Elvira groaned. "Now I am confused."

"That's a first," Mercedes joked.

Elvira shot her a dirty look and ignored the comment. "Check it out. The other guy looks a lot like Towns."

Carlita studied the backs of the men standing at the bar. They were the same height, build and had the same hair color. From their vantage point, it was hard to tell which one was Quinton Towns.

"This meeting was no coincidence," Elvira commented.

"How do you figure?" Annie asked.

"Body language. You gotta study the body language." Elvira pointed at two empty barstools toward the center of the bar. "Why didn't the guy take one of those seats? He walked to the other end for a reason." She reached for a chip, scooped some salsa on it and shoved it into her mouth.

The newcomer turned to study the bar crowd. "There's something about the man...the second man. He looks familiar," Elvira said through her mouthful of food. "I know I've seen him before."

"I was going to say the same thing." Annie nibbled on the side of her chicken wing. "It could be I've seen him on television."

"No." Elvira shook her head. "I mean, maybe he's been on television. I've seen him somewhere else. I never forget a face."

"Oh. I know who he is." Annie scooched forward. "He's one of the Savannah city commissioners. I think his name is Pridgen something."

"That's it," Elvira hissed. "His name is Emmett Pridgen. He's been on the news lately, spearheading a large project near the riverfront. They're trying to convert one of the old shipping yards into some sort of entertainment complex."

"Yes, that's right," Annie said. "I've been keeping up on the story since this project could be huge for the Savannah area. There's talk of polling county residents to see if they're interested in introducing gaming lounges."

"G...gaming lounges?" Carlita stuttered.

"Riverboat casinos, like they do in some of the other states. Gambling would be big business for the Savannah area. From what I've heard, some of the city officials are against it, claiming it would attract an unsavory crowd."

Carlita's head began to spin and the pieces began to fall into place. Vito Castellini's comment to Vinnie, asking if he'd taken care of business. Vinnie taking over the casino in Atlantic City. Castellini just so happened to be in town to take care of other business.

This was exactly what Carlita was looking for...the link between bookie Robert, the wads of cash in the backpack, the Harner Street property, how Tony mentioned he thought the tunnel beneath the property Robert owned led to the river.

Was it a coincidence Robert died around the same time Vinnie and Castellini breezed into town? Elvira swore she saw Vinnie in front of the Black Stallion talking to someone. Was it Robert? Did her son meet with Robert and then kill him?

Mercedes squeezed her mother's arm under the table. Casinos meant mafia, at least it did up north. "We need to take a picture of these men."

"Make it look natural," Annie sprang from the chair and grabbed Carlita's elbow. "Where should we stand?"

Mercedes shifted to the right. "A little more that way and...perfect. Let me get one more shot." She snapped another photo with her cell phone and slipped it back into her purse. "Not sure who the dude is behind the counter, but he and the other two are on the move."

"They're heading to the john." Elvira shoved her chair back and scrambled around the table.

"Where are you going?" Mercedes asked.

"To the men's restroom."

"You can't go in there," Carlita gasped.

"Why not? I bet I can walk right in there and no one is going to stop me."

"Unless some guy decides he doesn't want a female standing next to him at the urinal and pops you," Annie said.

"It's a possibility," Elvira shrugged.

"Not to mention, if you make a scene the bouncers are going to throw us out," Carlita pointed out.

"Don't do it," Mercedes warned.

"All right." Elvira rolled her eyes. "Chillax. I'll go hang out in the hall. Watch and learn."

She sauntered to the back of the bar and casually leaned against the wall directly across from the restrooms. Elvira pulled her cell phone from her purse and began studying the screen.

The man now identified as Emmett Pridgen exited the bathroom. Instead of returning to the bar, he turned right and disappeared from sight.

Elvira gave the women a thumb-up and then followed Pridgen down the hall.

"Oh my gosh. She's following him," Annie gurgled.

"I would say I'm surprised, but I'm not," Carlita said. "Get ready. We might have to make a quick exit."

Thankfully, the server returned with Carlita's card and receipt. She hastily scribbled in a generous tip and signed the bottom.

Several more men entered the hall, passed by the restroom and disappeared from sight.

"Where are they going? Where is Elvira?" Carlita's armpits grew damp as visions of an injured Elvira filled her head.

There was a small commotion near the back hall. Elvira and two burly bouncers appeared. The bouncers began dragging Elvira across the dance floor.

"Take your hands off of me! I'm perfectly capable of exiting this disgusting dive on my own two feet!"

The men ignored Elvira's protests and continued escorting her to the exit.

"Let's go." Annie, Mercedes and Carlita bolted from the table and hurried after them.

By the time they exited the club, Elvira was standing on the sidewalk. "You have no right to manhandle me like that. I ought to file a police complaint."

One of the bodyguards took a menacing step towards her. "You entered a restricted area and were asked to leave. Since you ignored our request, we escorted you out. If you ever set foot inside the Black Stallion again, we'll have you arrested."

"Oh, you won't have to worry about me setting foot inside this dump ever again." Elvira lifted her middle finger and waved it in the air.

The other man made a move toward Elvira and she ran down the sidewalk.

The trio jogged along behind Elvira, joining her a safe distance from the club.

"No one has a sense of humor these days."

"What were you doing back there?" Annie asked.

"At first, I thought something funny was going on inside the men's restroom, but when I got there, I realized all of these patrons were bypassing the toilet and entering a room in the back."

"So you decided to see what they were up to," Mercedes prompted.

"Yeah. I figured it was worth a shot. I made it as far as the doorway when one of the goons escorted me out. I asked him what was going on and he said something about it being a private party. He grabbed my arm. I tried to pull away and out of nowhere comes goon number two. Next thing I know, they're dragging me out of the bar."

"So you weren't able to see what was going on in the back?"

"You underestimate the determination of Elvira Cobb when she's on a case. Before I was manhandled, I got a peek inside the room, and you'll never guess what's going on in the Black Stallion Club."

Chapter 23

Elvira lowered her voice. "Illegal gambling. I saw a roulette wheel and a craps table. There were a bunch of men off to the side, and I think I saw them playing cards before the creeps shut me down."

"I wish I coulda snapped a picture, but the goons were on me too fast." Elvira began walking and the others hurried to keep up.

"I appreciate you trying to help us, Elvira," Carlita said as she fell into step with her former tenant. "I'm still trying to figure out why you put yourself in harm's way this evening."

"I already told you...I wanted to know who the mystery man was. I don't like people lurking in our neighborhood. After you told me that someone broke into Shelby's apartment, I figured we needed to find out whom we were dealing with. Plus, I like Shelby and Violet."

"Huh." Carlita shoved her hands in her jacket pockets. "So you've been doing all of this for the safety and security of our neighborhood?"

"Absolutely. Not to mention I have a little free time on my hands. The security services business is booming. The investigative business is a little slow right now. Robert Towns' death is all over the news. If Emmett Pridgen is involved, we could be hot on the trail of one of the biggest news stories Savannah has seen in decades."

"Ah." Carlita nodded. "Now I get it. If this turns out to be a big news story, Elvira Cobb and EC Investigative Services will get plenty of free advertising."

Mercedes chuckled. "And here we thought you were doing this out of the goodness of your heart."

"It's a little of both," Elvira admitted. "Nothing wrong with that."

"I wish we could've eyeballed the owner of the Black Stallion, Pat Duce," Carlita said.

Elvira abruptly stopped. "Are you saying the owner of that dump is someone by the name of Pat Duce?"

"Yeah," Annie said. "We looked it up before we left."

"While I was in the hall, one of the doofuses kept referring to someone named Duce. Next thing I know, there's some woman standing behind me. She was the one who told her goons to escort me out."

"She?" Mercedes asked. "Pat is a she?"

"Without a doubt." Elvira nodded. "She was dressed down, but judging by the body parts I observed, Pat Duce is definitely a woman."

"I'll be darned."

Elvira continued walking. "What do you plan to do with the information?"

"Shelby is coming for dinner. We're going to tell her what we found out and urge her to go down to the police station."

"It's a far-fetched story," Annie said. "Maybe you should go with her since you have more of the details."

Carlita's mind was whirling. How could she possibly explain her theory to the authorities? Would they even believe her? They would have to believe her. Her main concern now was informing the authorities without implicating Vinnie.

"I don't think we should wait, Ma. Tony and Shelby can take the deed, the backpack with the cash, the laptop and the pictures down to the station."

Elvira brightened. "You want me to go with them? I was the one who saw the gambling room."

"I don't think that will be necessary. Once Tony and Shelby fill the authorities in, they'll investigate," Carlita said.

"I wouldn't be so sure about that," Mercedes said. "Maybe Pridgen greased some palms, too, and the local authorities already know about the illegal gambling at the Black Stallion."

"True." They walked Annie to her car and waited for her to leave before heading across the street.

"I appreciate your offer, Elvira, I really do. I'll have Tony give the authorities your contact information in case they want to follow up," Carlita said.

Elvira seemed disappointed.

"I'm sorry. If it's any consolation, you've been a big help."

"All I ask is if you end up in front of a news crew, could you please throw out the EC Investigative Services' name a time or two?"

"I will. I promise."

"I once read if you repeat something three times, people have a much better chance of remembering it, so if you could say it three times, it would be even better."

Carlita chuckled. "Okay, Elvira. *If* I go to the station, and *if* I run into reporters, I'll try to repeat EC Services' name three times, but don't get your hopes up. There's a chance this story won't even make the news."

"Corrupt politicians," Elvira mumbled.

Carlita was still smiling when Elvira entered her building and slammed the door shut. "Some things never change." She turned to her daughter. "Let's track down Tony and Shelby."

***

Violet stayed with Carlita at the apartment while Tony and Shelby gathered up the evidence and drove to the police station.

It seemed as if they were gone forever and the hands on the clock crawled.

Brittney and Vinnie arrived and began helping Carlita set the dinner table.

"Vinnie, could grab the silverware? I'm going to send Tony a quick text." Carlita had just picked up her cell phone when she heard a muffled *thump*. The door flew open and Tony and Shelby stepped inside.

"Thank goodness," Carlita hurried to the door. "I was getting worried. How did it go?"

"Better than expected. We gave the authorities the proof that Robert owned the Harner Street property, I turned over the backpack with the laptop, showed them the bookie website and the envelope filled with the cash."

Mercedes wandered over. "Did you tell them about the illegal gambling at the Black Stallion?"

Vinnie dropped the fork he was holding. "Who said there was illegal gambling at the Black Stallion?"

"Violet, why don't you let Rambo out onto the deck?" Mercedes waited until the child was out of earshot.

"What about the killer?" Mercedes asked.

"I think they're hot on the trail of Pridgen and Duce," Tony said.

"What about the brother, Quinton?" Carlita asked.

"The authorities plan to question him, too," Shelby said. "My personal opinion is that I think Quinton was in on the gambling ring, but that was the extent of his involvement. He knew about the money, but not about the property. The brothers had a strange relationship."

"There's also the illegal gambling operation in the back room of the Black Stallion," Carlita pointed out.

"We tried to tell the authorities about that. They blew it off. I think the officials already know and are turning a blind eye," Tony said.

"That's wrong," Mercedes said.

"It happens all of the time," Vinnie spoke up. "You would be surprised."

"Now that the unpleasantness is behind us," Tony said as he turned to Brittney. "Brittney, I don't think you've met my girlfriend, Shelby."

Shelby shyly extended her hand and Brittney took it, giving her a warm smile. "It's so nice to meet you. Do you like to shop?"

Mercedes laughed. "Oh no. That's a loaded question."

Violet skipped back into the room and her mother helped her into her chair.

Carlita waited until everyone was seated before taking her place at the head of the table.

Despite Vinnie's shocking news of his recent nuptials, and to a mafia boss' daughter no less, she was happy for her son.

It appeared Tony and Shelby had overcome their first major crisis and were back on track.

Tony tapped the side of his glass with his fork. "Shelby and I have an announcement." He turned to Shelby. "Go ahead, show them."

"Show us what?" Carlita asked.

Shelby held up her hand, revealing a glittering diamond engagement ring. "Tony proposed to me a few moments ago."

"You did?" Carlita began jumping up and down. "You're engaged. Oh my gosh."

The table erupted in excited chatter as everyone congratulated the newly engaged couple.

"This is the best news I've heard in a long time," Carlita gushed and then caught Vinnie's eye. "Other than the wonderful news of Vinnie and Brittney's marriage."

Carlita admired the ring. "It's time to plan a wedding. Promise me you won't run off and elope like your older brother."

"Not a chance," Tony grinned. "We're gonna do it up big."

When the excitement over Tony and Shelby's announcement died down and everyone began eating, Carlita paused to gaze at her loved ones seated at the table.

As far as she knew, Paulie and Gina were on solid ground. The only one left was Mercedes, who dated here and there. So far, she hadn't shown a strong interest in any of the men she'd met.

Mercedes reached for another slice of crusty bread. "Don't look at me like that Ma."

"Like what?"

"Like you're trying to find me a husband or something. I know that look."

Tony snorted and Vinnie laughed. "You know Ma would never try to play matchmaker," Tony teased.

"I would not," Carlita said.

"Ma..." Tony smiled.

"Okay. Maybe a little, but you and Shelby were such a perfect match. Now eat your food before it gets cold and leave your poor mother alone."

***

Vinnie helped his wife into the car and then closed the door. He joined his mother near the back. "It was nice seein' you, Ma. As soon as our apartment is ready and we're situated, you'll have to come up for a visit."

"I will, Vin." Carlita nodded toward the car. "I like Brittney. She's a sweet person. I hope you have a long and happy marriage."

"And lots of children," Vinnie joked.

"That too. I'm not sure about six, though."

"Eh. We'll work it out." Vinnie changed the subject. "You hear anything back from Tony on Shelby's ex?"

"Yeah. Tony called before I went to bed last night. The authorities brought Quinton in for questioning. According to what the investigators told him, someone had used Quinton as a punching bag."

"Someone beat the brother up?" Vinnie asked.

"Yeah, they got him good," Carlita nodded. "When the authorities told Quinton that eyewitnesses placed him inside the Black Stallion Club earlier in the evening, he confessed he'd been worked over by some people his brother owed some money to."

Carlita continued. "After more questioning, Quinton also confessed he broke into Shelby's apartment, looking for a backpack and money Robert owed to some 'associates.'"

"Did he say who those associates were?"

"Yeah. Quinton said it was Pat Duce and some other individuals who frequented the club," Carlita replied. "I figured he would name Pridgen, but Quinton claims the only thing he knew about Pridgen was that he had some business dealings with the Black Stallion Club."

"So you're thinking Pat Duce killed Robert?"

Carlita nodded. "Quinton swears Duce hired someone to murder Robert. She told Quinton that if he didn't come up with the cash, he would meet the same fate as his brother. Quinton cut a deal to cooperate with authorities in exchange for immunity."

"What about the illegal gambling?"

"Tony said they charged Duce with Robert's murder and shut down the Black Stallion Club."

Carlita lifted a brow. "Why? You concerned about future business transactions?"

"Nah. Vito visited the Black Stallion Club while he was here. He said it was small potatoes, although he is interested in possibly expanding his operations."

"Gambling," Carlita guessed.

"That is one of his lines of business."

Carlita walked Vinnie to the driver's side of the car. "I'm gonna miss you son."

Vinnie noted the look of concern in his mother's eyes. "Don't worry Ma. Like I said, Vito isn't such a bad guy."

"So you say."

Vinnie hugged his mother tightly and then reached for the door handle. "I'm sure you'll be planning a big wedding for Shelby and Tony."

"Yeah, since I got ripped off with yours."

"I feel kinda guilty about that."

"You should."

Vinnie opened the car door and climbed inside. "Brittney and I already decided we're gonna come back down for the grand opening of Ravello."

"You are?" Carlita brightened. "I can't wait." She impulsively leaned in and kissed her son's cheek. "Now try to stay out of trouble...both of you." She winked at Brittney.

"And I could say the exact same thing for you," Vinnie shot back.

"The Garlucci family stay out of trouble?" Carlita rolled her eyes. "We'll have to see about that."

The end.

If you enjoyed reading "The Family Affair," please take a moment to leave a review. It would be greatly appreciated. Thank you.

The series continues...book 10 in the "Made in Savannah Cozy Mystery" series coming soon!

Books in This Series

Made in Savannah Cozy Mystery Series

Get Free eBooks and More

Sign up for my Free Cozy Mysteries Newsletter to get free and discounted ebooks, giveaways & soon-to-be-released books!

hopecallaghan.com/newsletter

Meet the Author

Hope loves to connect with her readers! Connect with her today!

Visit **hopecallaghan.com/newsletter** for special offers, free books, and soon-to-be-released books!

Email: hope@hopecallaghan.com

**Facebook:
https://www.facebook.com/authorhopecallaghan/**

Hope Callaghan is an author who loves to write Christian books, especially Christian Mystery and Cozy Mystery books. She has written more than 50 mystery books (and counting) in five series.

In March 2017, Hope won a Mom's Choice Award for her book, "Key to Savannah," Book 1 in the Made in Savannah Cozy Mystery Series.

Born and raised in a small town in West Michigan, she now lives in Florida with her husband.

She is the proud mother of one daughter and a stepdaughter and stepson. When she's not doing the thing she loves best - writing books - she enjoys cooking, traveling and reading books.

Tuscan Chicken Macaroni and Cheese Recipe

<u>Ingredients</u>:

2 large skinless boneless chicken breasts pounded to 1-inch thickness (or 4 boneless and skinless chicken thigh fillets)

Salt and pepper, to season

1/2 teaspoon paprika

3 teaspoons olive or canola oil, divided per directions

2 tablespoons butter

1 small yellow onion chopped

6 cloves garlic, finely diced

1/3 cup chicken broth

4 oz (250g) sun dried tomato strips in oil (reserve 1 tablespoon of oil)

4 level tablespoons flour

2 cups chicken broth

3 cups milk OR light cream

2 teaspoons dried Italian herbs

10 ounces (3 cups) elbow macaroni uncooked (3 cups)

3/4 cup freshly grated Parmesan cheese

1 cup mozzarella cheese shredded (or use six cheese Italian)

2 tablespoons fresh basil, chopped

Directions:

-Season chicken with salt, pepper, paprika and 2 teaspoons of the oil. Heat the remaining oil in a large pot or pan over medium-high heat. Add the chicken and sear on both sides until golden brown, cooked through and no longer pink in the middle. Transfer chicken to a warm plate, tent with foil and set aside.

-Using the same pan, add the butter and fry the onion and garlic until the onion becomes transparent, stirring occasionally (about 2 minutes). Pour in the 1/3 cup chicken broth and allow to simmer for 5 minutes, or until beginning to reduce down.

 -Add the sun dried tomatoes, along with 1 tablespoons of the sun dried tomato oil from the jar. Cook for 2-3 minutes.

 -Stir the flour into the pot. Blend well.

-Add the broth, 2-1/2 cups of milk (cream or half and half), herbs, salt and pepper, and bring to a low simmer.

-Add the uncooked macaroni and stir occasionally as it comes to a simmer. Reduce to medium low heat and stir regularly while it cooks (roughly 10 minutes), or until the sauce thickens and the macaroni is just cooked (al dente: tender but still firm).

-Remove pot from stove and immediately stir in all of the cheeses. Add salt and pepper to taste. If the sauce it too thick, add the remaining 1/2 cup milk (or cream) in 1/4 cup increments, until reaching desired thickness.

-Slice the chicken into strips and stir through the pasta (pour in any juices left from the chicken).

-Sprinkle with basil, stir thoroughly and serve.

Made in the USA
Columbia, SC
24 March 2025

55632889R00188